Co. 2

FIC   Chayefsky, Paddy
Cha   Altered states.

Altered States

Paddy Chayefsky

ALTERED STATES

A NOVEL

HARPER & ROW, PUBLISHERS
NEW YORK, HAGERSTOWN, SAN FRANCISCO, LONDON

1-87 gift Co. 2

For my wife, Susan
For my son, Dan

Contents

Bethesda, Maryland: 1965   1

New York, Nairobi, Simla, Boston: 1967–1975   7

Zapatecus, Mexico: June 1975   45

Boston: Harvard Medical School, Peter Bent Brigham
Hospital: October 1975–January 1976   57

Cambridge, Harvard Medical School, Van Buren Park
Zoo: April 1976   93

Cambridge, Harvard Medical School: April–May 1976   139

Beacon Hill: May 1976   165

Acknowledgments   183

Bethesda, Maryland
1965

The isolation tank itself was nothing more than a coffin-like bathtub made of plywood and lined with aluminum, eight by eight by ten feet and half filled with a 10 percent solution of magnesium sulfate in water to increase buoyancy. The water was heated to 93°F, the temperature at which a floating body feels minimal gravity. Every morning, a volunteer from Andrews Air Force Base came by, stripped and stood there while a medical student from Johns Hopkins took blood samples and Jessup wired him up to all the EEG and EKG equipment. Heart rate, pulse, blood pressure and galvanic skin response were tested. After this preparation, the subject climbed into the tank and floated. Jessup and his assistant placed the lid on the tank and went off to the monitoring room. Inside the tank, the volunteer subject floated in utter darkness and utter silence, effectively deprived of sensory stimulation, alone, isolated.

In the beginning, it had been presumed that being entombed in a black, silent, coffinlike contraption would induce paranoia, certainly anxiety. But, on the whole, that didn't happen. In Jessup's two years in Bethesda, only five of the sixty-two subjects showed signs of anxiety and opened the hinged lid and asked to be dropped from the experiments. The others reported experiences ranging from pleasant to exhilarating. It seemed that depriving a man of external stimuli simply triggered a whole new set of internal stimuli. All the subjects, including those who dropped out, reported early disturbance in temporal and spatial orientation. The sense of confinement disappeared quickly, and after half an hour, the subjects couldn't tell if they had been in the tank ten minutes or two hours. Most of the subjects reported intense sensory excitement, especially in the area of sexual fantasy. Several even achieved orgasm. Forty-nine of the subjects had hallucinatory experiences, and almost all reported increased clarity of mental processes and even new patterns of thinking. That is to say, their thinking, normally linear and logical, became holistic and patterned. They saw things as a gestalt rather than in specifics. Some were able to do complicated algebra problems instantly, problems that would ordinarily have required a step-by-step solution. The most common reaction was a deep sense of rest and refreshed energy. This was supported by the electroencephalographic evidence. The first phase was marked by a distinct, repeated pattern of change. Within minutes after the activating period, well-organized alpha waves of 40–50μV, 11–12/sec., appeared in all regions. After fifteen minutes, there was an increase in alpha amplitude, as much as 30–70μV, predominantly in the frontal and central regions. At the half-hour mark, rhythmical waves of 7–8/sec. appeared, and then, suddenly, rhythmical theta trains (6–7/sec., 70–100μV) began to appear. This EEG pattern was startlingly similar to that of Zen priests in meditation.

At any rate, on November 19, 1965, Jessup decided to take a shot at going into the tank himself. His series of experiments for NASA were over. He was writing up his findings now. The tank wasn't being used. At 11:30 A.M. on that day, he went down to the tank room, filled the tank with three feet of water, checked the temperature gauges, stripped off his clothes, climbed into the tank, pulled the hinged lid back over himself, lay back and floated in the black, confined silence.

At first, there were a number of physical distractions. He was fearful his head would sink, and some water got into his ears. His toes and fingers began to wrinkle. He poked about with his feet, causing ripples, hanging on in a strangely frightened way to the last bits of external sensation. He had some trouble finding a comfortable position and finally settled on folding his hands behind his head. He was conscious of the intense confinement of the walls all around him, but mostly he was startled by the utter blackness. Even in the darkest rooms, one always expects one's eyes to adjust and to find some light. But there was absolutely no light here, nothing for his eyes to adjust to. It was relentlessly black and suddenly silent. The abrupt rush of silence was shocking, palpable, alive. He felt fear. Nobody knew he was here; suppose he couldn't get the lid off. There were only three feet of water in the tank, but he was no longer sure of that. He had the feeling he was floating in bottomless blackness. He had the feeling he was suffocating. He had the feeling he was drowning. Panic tore out of his deepest self and swept over his white, naked, floating body. Then, as suddenly, it was gone, as though washing out into the water around him. He could almost envision his fears liquefied, greenish in color, occasionally viscid, oozing out of his white body into the water. He was abruptly aware he was seeing now in the utter blackness. In fact, there was a great deal of light, almost a radiance. The wooden grains of the black walls of the tank behind the aluminum lining took on living forms. He suddenly saw an image of a green veronica, one of those religious handkerchiefs with the face of Christ painted on it, chalk white with little red kewpie spots on the cheeks, a crown of thorns on the brow. In an instant, he saw an infinite expanse of surrealist landscape, stretches of brilliantly white beach on which his naked body lay thickly, blackly outlined in ink. My God, he thought to himself, I'm hallucinating.

It was of interest that despite the hallucinatory experience, he was not losing his rational awareness. He was Edward Jessup lying naked in an isolation tank in Bethesda, Maryland, and he was hallucinating. He wondered what the precise physiological activities must be to produce a hallucination. A page of a medical textbook popped up on a computer screen in front of him on which was printed: "Visual displays are caused by spontaneous excitation of parts of the brain." It seemed a remarkably pompous statement. Suddenly, everything was red, the color of rage. He felt himself shouting: "What parts of the brain? What the hell are you talking about?" Then he saw an image of a cluster of neurons, sleeping neurons, actually curled up in postures of sleep, lying in subdued shadow. The implication was clear. These were stored neurons, stored in some bank of our mental computers, perceptions picked up somewhere in life and selectively filtered out of our rational consciousness, the stuff of dreams. They were waiting to be activated, to be fired.

One thing seemed immediately, shatteringly clear. Aside from the beach hallucination, his imagery was of a physiological nature. Apparently, one brings into the hallucination the constructs of one's ordinary life. He was a physiologist; therefore, his hallucinations would be within physiological forms. He was looking at his own brain now, moving into the grayish masses of thundering neurons, concerned for the moment with a curious contradiction. Since his hallucinations and his awareness of the hallucinations were both products of his own brain, how could one detachedly observe the other, especially as his self-awareness was now taking the shape of a swollen, obviously aroused vagina, into which his whole body was plunging with trembling anticipation. The vagina changed to a very realistic, extraordinarily eidetic image of a faceless yet somehow beautiful young woman back on the eternally white beach writhing in sexual exuberance, and he was there on the beach, writhing with her in totally uncharacteristic abandon, wildly, freely, heedlessly, violently, thrusting at her, in her. He noted that the face of the girl was the face of Jesus Christ, the one on the veronica, but now distorted in sensual pleasure, despite the crown of thorns still on his brow. With a flash of red brilliance, Jessup exploded into orgasm. He was suddenly back in the black, silent tank, floating effortlessly, serene, peaceful and hooked.

He stood up in the three feet of water and pushed up at the hinged lid. It opened with no trouble at all. Dripping wet, he clambered out of the tank and into the dark, sound-attenuated room. His clothes and a bath towel were in the corner of the room where he had put them. He dried himself languorously. After a few moments, he felt ready to click on the soft lights of the room and return to external reality. He felt very pleased with himself, singularly voluptuous. He enjoyed toweling himself very much. He fetched his wrist watch out of his jacket pocket, tried to read the time in the subdued light. It appeared to read 5:42. That didn't make sense; so he unlocked the door of the tank room and walked, oblivious of his nakedness, into the lighted corridor outside and looked at his watch again. It was 5:43. He had been in the tank for more than six hours. It was extraordinary.

New York, Nairobi, Simla, Boston
1967–1975

Emily Jessup first met her husband in New York at a party in Arthur Rosenberg's house. That was in the fall of 1967. Rosenberg, newly married, was living in a three-room flat at Ninety-seventh Street and West End Avenue, and the gathering was one typical of young intellectuals: subdued Janis Joplin on the stereo and joints being passed around. There were two biochemists, a geneticist, one pregnant painter (Mrs. Rosenberg), one sculptor, a pharmacologist (Rosenberg), one physical anthropologist, and one psycho-physiologist. The physical anthropologist was Emily, then doing postgraduate work under Holloway at Columbia. She had, in point of fact, just handed in her doctoral dissertation and was sweating out the response of the committee. She was twenty-four years old, and a very pretty twenty-four, cropped blond hair and hip-hugging jeans, a leggy, confident young woman. Anthropology seems to attract good-lookers. The psychophysiologist was Edward Jessup, then twenty-eight years old, middling height, slight of frame, flaxen-haired, fine, intense features, pale complexion. He wore gold-rimmed glasses which pinched his face and gave him a look of Calvinist austerity. Emily thought him very attractive in a monkish way. He had just got his doctorate and was teaching physiology at the Cornell Medical College. He was doing some work on schizophrenics with Rosenberg and a clinical psychiatrist named Hobart at Payne Whitney. And he and Rosenberg were also doing some moonlighting research of their own in sense deprivation and isolation. Emily had had her eye on him for some time. He had parked himself in a corner of the living room couch at nine o'clock and had had almost nothing to say all evening. She squeezed in beside him and said, "Arthur says you're very shy, and he wants me to draw you out."

"Draw me out?" said Jessup. "Doesn't sound like Arthur."

"As a matter of fact," said Emily, "what he said was that you were an arrogant, high-handed prick, a little bonkers, but you're absolutely brilliant. He said you and he were into sensory deprivation and isolation tanks and that you were probably doing the only serious work in the field, that you had worked out the beginnings of a quantifiable methodology for studying interior experiences. He said you were probably the hottest physiologist in town, and that you had offers from Harvard, Michigan and Stanford, and that if

I could ever get you talking, I would find you fascinating."

Jessup nodded. "That sounds more like Arthur."

And that seemed to be the end of that. He folded his hands in his lap and stared at them. She asked him what sort of work he and Rosenberg were doing at Payne Whitney. He said, "Toxic metabolite stuff. We're more or less replicating Heath's and Friedhoff's strategies, trying to find maverick substances specific to schizophrenia. I think we're chasing our tails, looking for a single etiologic agent produced by a single pathogenic mechanism." He had said all this as if she was expected to know what he was talking about. She told him she hadn't understood a word he had said. "Well," he sighed, clearly reluctant to go on, "we're trying to establish that schizophrenia has a physiology different from normals. I have no argument with that. Lord knows there's a ton of evidence to support that. I just don't think transmethylation is the process by which to find this out, and I don't think schizophrenia can be reduced to a single agent. Look, you're not really interested in this, because Lord knows I'm not. I suspect that when Arthur says you would find me interesting, he was really referring to the work we're doing in sense deprivation and isolation tanks. Would you like to hear about that?"

"Yes," she said.

"I'm not comfortable at parties," he said. "Would you like to go somewhere and have a cup of coffee?"

They went to a coffee shop at Eighty-sixth and Broadway. Jessup told her how he had got into isolation studies, which he had always considered pretty flaky stuff and still did. By his own admission, he was as square as they came, strictly establishment, a straight, lab-oriented scientist. He had originally intended to work in hemispheric dominance; he had hoped to join Sperry and his group at the University of California. Then he was suddenly given the chance to do his doctorate under Gregory Hayworth, who was head of the Behavioral Services Department for NASA. Hayworth was doing a series of studies in stress under conditions of isolation. The space program was naturally interested in the psychological states its astronauts would experience, capsuled in small spaces for long periods of time, and it was giving out grants by the bushelful. You don't get too many chances to work with someone like Hayworth, and the grant was a beauty, so the next thing Jessup knew, he was down in Bethesda, Maryland, in an outbuilding of the National Institutes of Health, working with an isolation tank.

He met Arthur Rosenberg in Bethesda. Rosenberg was working right across the street in the NIMH, studying the effects of LSD on schizophrenics. This was back in 1964, when LSD was still considered an interesting therapeutic drug and available for responsible research. Jessup was struck by the similarity between the tank experience and the psychotomimetic experience of LSD and other psychedelic drugs. He looked around for literature on the subject. There wasn't much work being done in isolation and sense deprivation, most of it brainwashing studies which the Army funded in the wake of the Korean War, but there was a voluminous, even chaotic, literature on LSD, some fifteen hundred papers. The experiences of LSD subjects are anarchically variable, he told Emily. Some subjects see things brilliantly illuminated, some subjects see everything shrouded in gloomy shadows. Some people are exhilarated, some feel paranoid. Some people recall things lost in their consciousness, some people see projections of the future. Some people don't feel anything at all. It was clear that the big problem with research in interior experience and altered states of consciousness was its total subjectivity and the fact that the communication between subject and observer frequently deteriorated. A subject is induced into altering his normal consciousness in an isolation tank or by a pharmacological agent or by hypnosis or self-induced trance, and his experiences are entirely personal, in fact, suprapersonal. The visions, hallucinations, distortions and deformities of cognition are his entirely, and he frequently cannot communicate them at all; and when he does communicate them, they frequently cannot be understood by the experimenter-observer he is communicating them to. Nor is there any way of knowing whether the information being communicated by a subject on an inner high is true or valid or accurately reported. The experimenter has no way of repeating them to check them out.

It seemed to Jessup that the whole world of inner and other consciousness was being improperly explored. The work being done in it was all radical stuff, an outgrowth of the contentious sixties, polemical in nature, a reaction against the establishment psychology of the times, tinged by Timothy Leary messianism. There were some good people working in the field, Tart, Ornstein, Deikman, but most of the literature was political rather than scientific, more interested in attacking Jensen and the behaviorists and Western science, exalting the irrational and intuitive over the rational and quantifiable. What had to be done, it seemed to Jessup, was to work out some kind of methodology for studying our other consciousnesses under controlled conditions. To that end, the isolation tank seemed the most effective device. Unlike the psychedelic drugs, volition is retained. The tank experience can be controlled, even programmed, by either the subject himself or the observer-experimenter. You can actually determine what inner space you want to get to. And unlike hypnosis, the subject is constantly aware. So in 1966, Jessup followed Rosenberg up to the Cornell Medical College in New York because it had an isolation tank in the basement. Every Wednesday night, he and Rosenberg took turns going into the tank. They were old pros at it by now. They had worked out half a dozen tank trips that either one of them could program himself into anytime he wanted to.

"What sort of programs?" asked Emily.

"Well, we have one trip that's a sort of ontogenetic demature. You program yourself back into your mother's womb and beyond that to the first cell of your conception. You can re-experience the explosion of your own birth. You sort of unfold all the layers of yourself back into the original cell. Arthur and I have replicated it. Would you like to hear some of our tapes?"

"I'd love to."

"The fact is, you ought to try a trip in the tank sometime."

"Terrific!"

"We've got another trip right down your alley. You program yourself back through collapsing veils of time into the fossilized bones of a protohuman creature, back into Pleistocene space. You can go hunkering along the savannas of primeval Africa."

"Fantastic," murmured Emily.

"There's method to it, you know. It isn't just freaking out. The first half hour, sometimes an hour, you spend achieving a state of suspension. You let your body unfold into the water, finding your moment of gravitylessness, feeling your body separate from the consciousness of the mind so that your body becomes a separate consciousness in itself and the consciousness of the body slowly subsides from the turbulence of rational awareness, until the silence is utterly soundless and the darkness utterly black and the sensed confinement of the wooden walls around you is spaceless and time disappears and all is one. This is a moment of total centeredness, lacking intelligence or will and consisting of nothing but essence. You're in the deepest theta you'll ever be in."

"Fucking fantastic," said Emily.

At 2 A.M., the manager of the coffee shop threw them out, and they went to Emily's place, a three-room flat on the third floor of a brownstone on 105th and Riverside Drive which she shared with another postgraduate student. They went into Emily's room, closed the door, and instantly ravened each other. It was an explosive experience for Emily. He went at her with the fervor of a flagellant, bucking into her with a coarse, almost fanatical zeal, which somehow seemed directed away from her. She had expected the fumblings of an inhibited scholar and instead found herself harpooned by a raging monk. She looked up at him in the middle and saw this white, ascetic face above her, eyes wide open, as if he were receiving God.

In a quiet moment between, in the dark room, resting among the rumpled sheets, she sitting up against the headboard, he sprawled belly-down across the bed, she studied his shadowed face. Even without his glasses, even with his eyes closed, almost asleep in post-coital repose, he seemed driven from within by some arctic passion. Rosenberg had told her he was a terrifically bright guy; she wondered if perhaps she wasn't looking at a shadow of genius.

"What do you think about when we're making love?" she asked him.

"God, Jesus, crucifixions."

"Well, as long as it isn't another woman," she said.

"I was a very religious kid," he mumbled into the sheets. He opened his eyes, lifted himself up on one elbow. "When I was nine, I saw visions, angels and saints, even Christ. He appeared to me in wonderful manners; I saw him with the eyes of faith, hanging on the cross, his vesture dipped in blood. I spoke in voices. There was this little Pentecostal church in south Yonkers that made a cult object of me. People came from all over to see this nine-year-old kid who saw visions of Christ."

"Is that where you're from, Yonkers?"

He turned on his back. "My mother still lives there. You'll have to meet her sometime. She's a clinical psychologist. My father's dead. He was an aeronautical engineer. Both of them were militant secularists. It appalled them to have a nine-year-old son who saw visions and spoke in voices. They had me round to every psychiatrist in Westchester County. When I was fifteen, I told my father that I had been called to the ministry and was applying to a divinity school. I thought he would cry. I was very fond of my father. He died when I was sixteen."

"How did a sixteen-year-old kid who saw visions wind up teaching physiology at the Cornell Medical School?"

"I stopped believing. It was very dramatic. My father died a protracted and painful death of cancer. I used to race to the hospital every day after high school and sit in his room doing my homework. He was very heavily sedated. The last few weeks he was in coma. One day I thought I heard him say something. I looked up. His lips were moving, but no sound came out. There was his yellow, waxen face on the white pillow, and his lips were moving. A little bubble formed on his lips. I got up and leaned over him, my ear an inch away from his lips. 'Did you say something, Pop?' I said. His lips moved again, and I could swear he was trying to say something, but there was no sound. I put my ear closer to his lips. Then I heard the word he was desperately trying to say, a soft hiss of a word. He was saying: 'Terrible —terrible!' So the end was terrible, even for the good people like my father. So the purpose of all our suffering was just more suffering. By dinnertime, I had dispensed with God altogether. I never saw another vision. I haven't told anybody about this in ten years. I'm telling you now because I want you to know what sort of a nut you might be getting mixed up with."

They stared at each other in the dark room. "Arthur was right," she said. "You are a fascinating bastard."

They embarked on a courtship. They went to a lot of

Third Avenue movies. Rosenberg talked them into marching in a Vietnam peace parade on Fifth Avenue. They lounged around the living rooms of other young academics, smoking grass and hash and listening to Jimi Hendrix. They saw each other almost daily. Jessup usually came by around lunch to pick her up at her office in Dodge Hall. They'd stroll across the campus to the Chock full o' Nuts on Broadway. One day, they strolled right through one of the campus riots that shook Columbia University in April of 1968, hardly noticing all the cops chasing all the college kids, indifferent to the fact that half the campus buildings had been occupied by rampaging students, leaning out the windows waving anarchist banners. They were both intensely work and career oriented. They talked about almost nothing else, even while they stood in line for movies or marched in peace parades or strolled across a riot-ridden campus; even in bed.

She went down to Payne Whitney once to see just what he and Rosenberg did with their schizophrenics, a disturbing experience for her. She joined Jessup behind a one-way screen from where they could observe the experimental room, an austere chamber with tiled floors and white walls and windows darkened by heavy steel mesh. Two naked bulbs hung from the high ceiling. An attendant brought in a young woman of twenty-five, wearing a johnny coat and foam-rubber hospital slippers. She had that singular razor-sharp look of madness and shuffled about giggling to herself. They put her down on a wooden chair in the middle of the room, and Hobart, the clinical psychiatrist, Rosenberg and a medical student, all in white lab coats, descended on her to take specimens of her blood, check her blood pressure and connect her up to an EEG machine. Hobart pulled up a second chair and asked her questions from a large loose-leaf notebook. She responded to nothing. She giggled and shuffled her feet and made small, senseless movements with her hands. "In a few minutes," Jessup explained to Emily, "they'll shoot 75 milligrams of dimethyltryptamine into her, and she'll trip out for about forty minutes. The change in her behavior will be noticeable." Indeed it was. Within a minute after injection, the mad girl stopped giggling and shuffling, closed her eyes and sat rigidly still as if in a trance. Hobart asked her his litany of questions from his notebook. She was responsive now, but when she was asked to perform simple tasks like drawing a triangle on a slate, she could manage only one leg of the triangle. Jessup suddenly left Emily's side and slipped into the experimental room to stand over the EEG machine, watching the fitful tracings of its stylus. A few moments later he was back.

"She's showing accelerated alpha rhythms," he said to Emily, "and intermittent alert patterns and other rhythmic patterns that pertain specifically to the limbic system. A number of our patients have these kinds of readings. It's hardly conclusive, but there does seem to be at least a flirting similarity between their EEG's and those of yogis in meditation and the subjects I've tested in the isolation tank, including my own. Suppose we stop thinking of schizophrenia as a disease and start to conceive of it as another and different state of consciousness. There is a striking preponderance of religious delusion among schizophrenics. In a few moments she'll start to talk, and in all probability she will tell us she is feeling some extraordinary communion with great and powerful metaphysical forces. She's always said something like that in the past."

As if on cue, the girl's voice suddenly announced over the audio speaker: "I feel like my heart is being touched by Christ."

Jessup started visibly. "Do you know," he said to Emily, "those are precisely the words I used to say when I was a kid seeing visions."

He turned abruptly and left the monitoring room, this time going out into the corridor. After a moment, she followed him. He was walking up and down the empty, yellow-walled corridor, deep in thought. He noticed her standing in the doorway and said, "What's fascinating about schizophrenics is that they are physically different. They are physically different from the rest of us, physically different from what they were before they became schizophrenic. They are more asymmetrical, have shorter anteroposterior diameters. They are more angular; their torsos are larger. They have different growth rates of hair, nail, epidermal and fibrous tissue. It's almost as if they were trying to change their physical selves to adapt to their different states of consciousness. This raises the hairy possibility that other states of consciousness can also be realized in different physical structures. That's a fucking hairy thought, isn't it?"

She nodded; it certainly was.

"You're a fruitcake, Eddie," she smiled.

He had been getting interested in Buddhism and yoga lately, ever since he had been struck by the similarity in encephalographic patterns between his own tank states and those of yogis and Zen monks in meditation. He was in correspondence with two young Indian physiologists at the University of Calcutta, G. K. Mishan and B. S. Chhan, who were doing EEG work on yogis. They were going to a lamasery north of Delhi that summer to do more intensive studies, and they had asked Jessup to join them. It was a Tibetan lamasery which had moved down into India after the Chinese invasion, an unusual opportunity to study Northern Yoga. The prospect fascinated Jessup. He had decided to go, though it would only be for the summer months. He had to be in Boston in September; he had been appointed to the faculty of the Harvard Medical School.

Sitting naked in her room while she stood naked behind an ironing board, he would tell her about Buddhism, at least about the perfunctory reading he had done in it. He was excited by Buddhism. For a godless man who had a compulsion for ultimacy, there was nothing like it. It is putatively a religion, he informed her, but there is very little divinity to it. There is no god, resurrected or not. It is the Self that contains immortality and ultimate truth. Man is the maker and master of his own fate. As man evolved biologically from the cells of the sea, so he evolves psychically to the ultimate Enlightenment, where he joins in Union with the Final and Original Consciousness. One achieves Enlightenment through yogic practices. Because Buddhism apotheosizes the Mind and Consciousness of man, yoga has to be considered a psychology, a purer psychology, in fact, than that found in the West. In the West, we don't really study the mind of man; we study the behavior of men. The Buddhist considers the everyday behavior of men to be a microscopic bit of their total consciousness. In fact, the Buddhist considers our mundane (or samsaric) self to be an interference to our eternal consciousness. The practices of yoga are designed to control our mundane, physical, samsaric selves in order to transcend them and to evolve to higher states of consciousness and self. To the yogi, then, our other states of consciousness are more valid and less illusory than our rational states, and he spends years learning techniques for getting into those other states. Jessup wanted to study these techniques. His primary interest in other consciousnesses was to develop a methodology for studying them, and he might as well start that summer with those technicians who had been doing it for two thousand years.

All this fitted in pretty well with Emily's own plans; she was no less intense about her work than was Jessup. She had her Ph.D. now, and she was scrounging around for a faculty job at one of the better universities. As soon as she learned Jessup was going to Boston in the fall, she began turning wheels to get on the Harvard faculty. Dangerfield, her adviser, was helping her out there, and it looked as if a job might come through. Meanwhile, Dangerfield thought she ought to do some post-doc work in Nairobi, where Louis Leakey was director of the Kenya national museum. As a matter of fact, she told Jessup as they twined around each other on her rumpled bed, she was frustrated as hell by the limitations of fossil evidence. She was, at that time, strictly a comparative anatomist, and her doctoral paper had been on the comparative cranial capacities of hominids and primates, but she had told Dangerfield she was starting to think all that body/brain stuff was rubbish. And Dangerfield had agreed. He was moving into behavioral anthropology himself and was beginning to hypothesize that the cortical changes that marked the emergence of man were probably more of a reorganization of the molar neural masses than an increase in cranial capacity. For God's sake, 450cc Australopithecines, the same cranial capacity as gorillas, had made tools. Anyway, Dangerfield had this eighty-thousand-dollar grant from the NSF, and he wanted her to go to Nairobi and do segmental cranial measurements, see if she couldn't find some microscopic tracings of blood vessels or sulci lines which might give them leads to possible changes in the cortical lobes. She'd get herself a room at the Hotel Ainsworth in Nairobi and start working on all that terrific material they had at Leakey's museum. Then, if her appointment to Harvard came through, she and Jessup could go to Boston together.

She was preposterously in love with Jessup. For all her hip cool, he could reduce her to tears, turn her into a sodden sulk of a woman unable to concentrate on anything; he could drive her to invent rages of jealousy that her own good sense told her were utterly unfounded simply by calling and saying he couldn't take her to lunch on a given day. She couldn't understand why she had suddenly gone nuts for this one particular physiologist. He made no effort to be liked. There were times when he seemed downright uncivil, but she learned after a while that he did not mean to be disagreeable. He simply didn't understand anything that didn't pertain to his work. He had minimal interest in art, politics, sports or people as such. He paid no attention to the academic intrigues, envies and spites that make up so much of the social world of scientists. He was, on the other hand, secretive and intensely competitive with scientists working in the same field as he. He rarely talked about his work; he regarded it as the most intimate part of him. That was how she knew she held a special place in his life, because he did talk to her. That was, in fact, the only expression of his feelings for her. There was no way she could induce him to say he loved her. He didn't understand the word, so he never used it.

"Whether you understand it or not," she complained more than once, "I'd just like to hear you say it."

"Why do we have to define our feelings at all?" he would answer. "Love is generally described as being a matter of electricity or magnetism or chemistry. Why not let it go at that? In fact, there's a fellow over in Yale named Burr who's doing some really fascinating work in what he calls life fields. Apparently, all living things give off an electrical aura that he actually measures on a voltmeter. Presumably, your aura and mine have some kind of electrical affinity for each other, a communal ionization. That fellow Burr is on to something there, I think. I've got a couple of his abstracts back at my place. I'll bring you one. It's intriguing stuff."

"Oh, Jesus!" she would sigh.

All his friendships were professional ones, and even these lasted only as long as they were useful to him. He was grossly exploitative, and he couldn't understand why she disapproved of that. It seemed only sensible to him to spend his time with people who had something to give him.

"But what are you giving to *them?*" she expostulated.

"I don't know. I can't imagine what it is that people see

in me. I think I'm very poor company. I occasionally wonder why you, for example, bother with me."

She had asked this of herself a thousand times—just what was it she was so helplessly in love with? The only answer that made any sense to her was his genius. If he wasn't already a certified one, he certainly had the makings. Everyone who knew him at all took it for granted he would make a big splash someday. His only discernible ambition was to eventually pick up a Nobel Prize, which he took as an inevitability. Everyone who knew him agreed. He had an extraordinary if monomaniacal mind. It was fascinating to watch him when something that was said caught a subterranean fancy of his. You could almost see his powerful intellect awaken, the tightening of its haunches, a predatory beast catching a scent. He would begin to ask poky little questions, questions that seemed to have very little relatedness to what was being said, but which eventually turned out to be remarkably pertinent, bits and pieces of some total pattern that had instinctually formed in his mind. His face would come alive as he pushed and probed with his questions, frowning if he thought the answers inadequate, scowling and blinking his eyes if he didn't get the point, grimacing if the victim of his questioning didn't see what he was driving at, exultant if it all suddenly fitted into place. He had an astonishing ability to absorb the most esoteric information and a merciless gift of finding the defective links in another scientist's reasoning, even if that scientist's discipline was light-years removed from his own field. But even more than his voracious intelligence, he had a quality that could only be called visionary. His mind would suddenly vault into untracked areas of speculation and he would give himself with abandon to outrageous and poetic hypotheses. On these occasions, she would literally feel chills go up and down her spine and a swift stirring of sensuality within her.

And just as well, for he was an inconsistent lover, to say the least. Not all their sex was the tumultuous experience of that first night. He was more often indifferent to her. Rosenberg once told her that among very religious Jews, the young men were encouraged to marry early to dispose of the lusts of the flesh so as to get on with the more significant business of studying Holy Law. She wondered if she didn't serve this purpose for Jessup. They made love when he felt like it, which was often enough, but these experiences more frequently than not had the quality of the lancing of a boil— abrupt, violent episodes. She would have preferred a little more serenity in the sack. Even so, she responded to him as with no other man. She was, at bottom, a solid, middle-class young woman from Nashville, whose father had a medical practice and whose mother belonged to all the local women's organizations, and her bourgeois soul was startled by the shocking sensations in her body. When the sex was good, it was very good; she had cascades of unbridled orgasms, almost profane in their physical extravagance.

At the same time, she was wretched and desperate. She confided to the Rosenbergs that she had to break off with Jessup, that this helplessness he had reduced her to was intolerable. She had always been her own woman, and she meant to stay that way. It was obvious, even to her, that Jessup didn't love her. He didn't love anything. He was incapable of love. He didn't relate to anything human. He was an alien here among us mortals, a man from Mars. She blamed it on his religiosity. The obsessed child of nine who saw visions of Christ was now the obsessed man who stared into space. If she had any brains at all, she sobbed to the Rosenbergs, she'd tell him to bugger off, then cry it out for a couple of weeks and be over it. She was frightened of him, constantly on her guard, afraid she might say something that would bring on that impatient scowl he gave to anything he thought trivial or silly. Normally a sociable young woman, she found herself isolated within the few friendships Jessup tolerated. Her life had simply been taken away from her. She felt humiliated, debased, exploited, enslaved. She would pace around her room at night sleepless and fuming, muttering and hissing out all the enraged things she wanted to tell him; but when she was with him, her purpose failed, and she was ashamed of her weakness, her cowardice. It couldn't go on this way. It had to come to a head.

One April afternoon, they sat on a bench in Riverside Park, surrounded by the brief spring effusion of dogwood blossoms.

"Listen," she said, "my parents and sister are coming up to visit me this weekend, and I'd like you to meet them."

He looked at her, genuinely puzzled. "Why?" he asked.

"Because I'm a nice Southern girl from Nashville, and nice Southern girls usually introduce the man they're going to marry to their family."

"How did marriage get into this?"

"Why the hell do you think I broke my back to get appointed to Harvard?"

"So we could be together in Boston."

"Yes! The implication—tenuous as it may have been— was that we would get married!"

"I don't see that necessarily follows. Why can't we just go on the way we are?"

She exploded. She stood and shouted: "What the hell do you want from me? I want a statement of intent right now! I want to know how important I am to you! Because I'm telling you right now I'm not going on the way we are! I'm not some cool chick who's in this just for the fucking! I don't go for all that cool stuff! With me, it's love and marriage and children and a home! That's the way I was brought up, and that's the way I am! I love you. I want to get married, and I want to know how you feel about that! I want a similar statement of intent right now!"

He took a few moments to consider this outburst. She felt foolish standing there stoking up her anger, so she sat. He finally said, "It would be a disaster, Emily."

She knew he would say something like that, but she was still unprepared for it. It took all her energy to keep from bursting into tears.

"I'm a solitary person, Emily," he went on. "You must know that. I need to be alone a great deal. I suspected this might come up sooner or later, so it's not that I haven't given some thought to it. I'm simply too selfish to be a husband and a father. I could take a crack at it, of course. If you insist on it, I'll try. I think of myself as a responsible person, and I certainly would try to do my best. But I would never believe in it, you see. Marriage would simply be a chore for me, like grading my students' papers or having to attend obligatory department meetings. I don't like teaching, if you follow my analogy, but I think I do it responsibly. But I don't like it, and I can't wait to get the chores over with so that I can get back to myself. And that's the sort of husband and father I would be. I would do all the things required of me, but only to get finished and done with them so I could get back to myself. I don't think you would accept that."

"No, I wouldn't," she murmured. Her entire body felt sore and swollen with sadness.

"You're the only person I've ever known I'm comfortable with," he said. "I think you understand me."

She frowned down at her hands, lying slackly in her lap. She sighed. "Well, that's it." She felt drained. "I do understand you, Eddie. Your trouble is you're still a religious freak. Everyday life has no reality for you at all. I don't have any reality for you. Nothing in the human condition has any reality for you because it's uncertain, imperfect, transient. You have to have some great immutable truth. You're still looking for God's truth, any truth, even a godless truth, as long as it's ultimate, absolute, permanent, everlasting. That's it, isn't it? I'm in love with an unfrocked priest, a renegade monk, a Faust freak who would sell his soul for the great truth. Well, human life doesn't have truth. We're born screaming in doubt, and we die suffocating in doubt, and human life consists of continually convincing ourselves we're alive. One of the ways we know we're alive is we love each other, like I love you. I know I'm alive right now because it hurts so goddamned much. But you saw the seventy-two faces of God when you were nine years old, and nothing less than that is going to satisfy you again. I'm never going to be anything more to you than a distraction. Oh, my God, I'm going to cry." She shielded her eyes but couldn't forestall the tears. She cried quietly.

"I admire you," he murmured, looking away. "I like being with you. I like making love to you. Isn't that enough?"

"I'm twenty-five years old," she mumbled between tears, "and it's not enough." She lifted her face, stared at the blue descent of dusk on the river. "It's a good thing we're splitting up for a while. You go to India, and I'll go to Africa, and maybe I can get over you. I've got to be loved back, Eddie. I'm not going to live the rest of my life with this kind of pain. I'll see you. Don't call me, okay? Let's say we're splitting up. Have a good time in India."

She stood and walked off down the park pathway heading for Riverside Drive. For a moment, Jessup half rose to follow her, and then sat back again on the bench and tried to feel a pain he didn't feel.

On May 17, Emily flew to London, where she stayed for several days going over some data with a friend who had been working with Napier in Ethiopia, and then flew on to Nairobi, where she plunged into her segmental cranial studies. They gave her a corner of an office in one of the low buildings behind the Kenya national museum, and she spent the bulk of her days hunched over a shoebox filled with skull fragments from Hominid 10 taken out of Olduvai Gorge. Fossil evidence comes in tiny bits of bone, and it's an arduous business trying to fit the fragments together. But despite the intense concentration required by the work, she would suddenly find tears filling her eyes and tracing wet courses down her cheeks, and she would just sit there with her arms hanging slackly into her lap.

Besides, she had begun to seriously question the validity of the work she was doing. Another visiting post doctorate fellow, a characteristically blond young Swede in open collar and safari shorts with whom she tried desperately to fall in love, persuaded her that the proper approach to threshold man was behavioral, not anatomical. He knew she was carrying a very heavy torch and convinced her she ought to put her calipers away and take a field trip of a few weeks to Jane Goodall's camp in Tanzania and have a look at Goodall's chimps. "You get over love affairs very quickly in the bush," he told her, "and you can start studying the behavior of other primates. Gives you some idea of what emergent man was like when he first ventured out of the forest." The idea appealed to her very much, and she packed a bag and took off for Goodall's camp, where she stayed ten days, crying in her tent every night. It was hopeless; she loved Jessup, and she wanted him, and she finally decided to go get him.

She jeeped back to Nairobi and took the first plane to Bombay and a connecting flight to Delhi, a very pretty twenty-five-year-old blonde in tight blue jeans, clutching a battered valise and toting a rucksack, not much different from the wild packs of American hippies who had made India their nation of that year and who cluttered the aisles of the planes. She slept fitfully throughout the long journey. At Delhi, she boarded the Kalka Mail for Simla, which was filled with dark-complected, hook-nosed Bengalis on their

way to Simla for a Kali ceremony. The shuddering blue
wooden carriages of her train climbed the precipitous ascent
into the Himalayas from the Gangetic plains, tottering
around one cliff after another. At a few minutes after two in
the afternoon of a baking hot August day, drenched with
sweat and in something close to a fever, she was in Jessup's
hotel, asking where he could be found. She was told he was
up farther in the hills, visiting a yogi. She left her valise and
rucksack with the concierge and followed a local boy up the
mountainside for an hour's climb. Exhausted, her hair plas-
tered in disarray across her blistering face, she finally hauled
herself onto a grassy ledge where an emaciated yogi in meditation sat perched in the traditional position at the entrance
to a cave. He had a little cushion under his rump, which
gave a forward pitch to his body, and concentrated his
glazed eyes on the dirt immediately in front of him. He also
had eight electroencephalographic leads issuing out of his
head, the wires trailing off to a portable EEG machine roost-
ing on spindly aluminum legs. Tending the machine were
Jessup in T-shirt and jeans and an Indian gent in a glaringly
white shirt, obviously one of Jessup's colleagues. She stared
at them for a moment and then sank onto her haunches, literally too tired to move another step. The black maw of the
cave, the weird yogi wearing only a lungi and with the wires
protruding from his head, a blood pressure cuff on his arm—
the whole tableau seemed threatening, nightmarish. Jessup
finally looked up and saw her. He was naturally startled. He
excused himself to his Indian colleague and shambled
slowly toward her. The sun was behind him, and his face

was shadowed, but then she saw he was smiling. She smiled in return. He held out a hand to help her to her feet.

"Come in the shade, for God's sake," he said.

"Do you still admire me?" she asked.

"Of course."

"Do you still find me sexy?"

"I'll always find you sexy," he said.

"Okay," she said. "I'll settle for that. Let's get married."

She rested her head on his shoulder. He embraced her. She had a vivid, piercing sensation of impending horror. She slumped against him in a dead faint. He gathered her up and carried her into the blackness of the cave.

They flew back to Boston on August 26, pausing in Amsterdam to get married, and by Labor Day they were settled into a four-room flat on Powell Street, the ground floor of one of those pretty four-story, red-brick, ivy-covered town houses in the Beacon Hill district.

They must have seemed a model young academic couple, he rattling off every morning in the Toyota to the Harvard Medical School, she trolleying out to Cambridge: bright, handsome young people. They taught, they researched, they published; Emily wrote a textbook, *Introduction to Anthropology*, which is, at this writing, the most widely adopted introductory text in its field. Their first child was born in 1970, a daughter named Grace, and then a second daughter, Margaret, in 1973. Jessup was made a full professor that year, and Emily an associate professor the year after. There was no lack of money. Between the two of them, they were taking down more than sixty thousand dollars a year. They had a summer cottage in Maine they were usually too busy to get to. Emily was now concentrating on the symbolic behavior patterns of savanna-living primates, her basic hypothesis being that the physical mechanisms for such symbolic behavior as speech were probably inchoate in the common primate ancestor of the Oligocene; and that these mechanisms evolved only in man because they were necessary to his survival as a hunting, meat-eating animal. Jessup had focused his research on the study of long-term memory.

He did some work with an endocrinologist named Mason Parrish on ACTH$^{4-7}$, a small chain of amino acids that seemed to be instrumental in instructing the memory mechanism to print short-term memory. Then a serendipitous thing happened to Parrish. He was called in to consult on a stroke patient with a Cushing syndrome at the Massachusetts General. The man had bursts of babbling, which, if you listened carefully, seemed to have the flavor of coherent, goal-oriented speech. Then someone recognized the speech as a Slovenian dialect. Parrish looked at the guy's chart; he was Irish on both sides and had never been out of Boston. They did a CAT scan and a cerebral arteriogram on the guy, and he had lesions in the anterior hippocampus and in the cyngulate gyrus, two organs of the limbic system. This was interesting because the limbic system is the earliest part of the forebrain to develop and is found even in such primitive animals as crocodiles. Parrish told Jessup about it because he knew Jessup was interested in oddball things like that. Jessup thought it sounded like an instance of prenatal recall. It certainly interested him, and he did a retrospective study of stroke and head trauma patients at the Massachusetts General in the previous ten years, looking for corroborative evidence. There was a better than random incidence of unusual and inexplicable recall. "Son of a bitch," said Jessup. "There may be some connection between lesions in the limbic system and memory." So he and a colleague in the Psychophysiology Department named Milton Mitgang gathered a group of patients on the neurology service and gave them batteries of tasks. The results showed that the short-term-memory task-acquisition ability is unimpaired by limbic lesions and that the short-term-memory function mechanisms remain intact. On the other hand, there was a significant memory decay, indicating that the limbic system does have some effect on laying down of long-term memory. But what effect? Jessup wanted to stimulate the areas that had been ablated by the lesions, but you can't stick microelectrodes into human cortices; so he got himself two graduate students and a sixty-five-thousand-dollar grant and went to work on rats, previously task-trained rats from the experimental-animal house. He was having good results. The experiments strongly suggested that stimulation of the limbic system revived long-term memory. At any rate, this was what he was working on in April 1975, when Arthur Rosenberg moved into the Boston area.

Rosenberg was by nature a sort of science bum. He had drifted around the country from Cornell to UCLA to the University of Chicago and then back to the Langley Porter Psychiatric Institute in San Francisco, latching on to any curious little research inquiry that caught his fancy. But he had a wife and two kids, and there's no money in random research, so he had got himself a teaching job at Boston U. and begun writing a pharmacology textbook to make money. On a Saturday afternoon in April, he and his wife, Sylvia, dropped in on the Jessups. They found Emily in a disheveled living room, hacking away on her typewriter. She rose with a shriek of delight, and there was considerable embracing. Jessup had gone off to the supermarket with the kids and his pal Mason Parrish; they were probably on their way back right now. Rosenberg went down to the street to wait for them. His first sight of Jessup in more than seven years was almost comically domestic. Jessup came ambling around the far corner, trundling his two-year-old daughter in a stroller with his left hand, holding a large brown paper bag of groceries with his right, while his five-year-old daughter hopped along behind him. At the same time, he was talking animatedly with a big, booming, full-bearded bear of a man in his mid-thirties, whom Rosenberg took to be Mason Parrish. It was a warm, bright afternoon, and the street was filled with kids on bicycles. Jessup and Parrish were both wearing Levi's and sweaters. It was too suburban for words. Jessup was even nodding to neighbors. Rosenberg couldn't resist smiling. "For God's sake," he said as they passed him. "If I didn't see it, I wouldn't believe it."

Jessup paused, stared at him, and said, "My God, Arthur! You're not supposed to be here till next week. Does Emily know you're here?"

"Sure. She's inside with Sylvia."

"My God! This is sensational! Mason, this is the Rosenberg I tell you about all the time."

Parrish, an ebullient good old boy from West Virginia,

grabbed Rosenberg's hand. "Hey, man!" he boomed, "it sure is!"

"Hey, man," said Rosenberg.

Jessup transferred his groceries to Parrish, unstrapped his two-year-old, fetched her across his shoulder and, hauling the stroller in his other hand, led the way up the stoop to his ground-floor apartment. The place was a scholarly shambles. Piles of books clotted the entrance foyer and were strewn around the floor in every room. Emily had set up a corner for herself in the living room, a bridge table for a desk, the typewriter barely visible among the welter of papers, periodicals, scholarly journals, students' theses that sometimes fluttered down onto the floor or into the several open cardboard cartons surrounding the table, which appeared to serve as Emily's filing system. Jessup had his own work corner in their bedroom, far more orderly: an honest three-drawer filing cabinet, an escritoire, thick hard-bound notebooks neatly labeled and shelved. But the rest of the room was in turmoil. Though it was nearly three o'clock, the large double bed was still unmade, and yesterday's clothing was flung over the backs of chairs or piled on the floor. Housekeeping was clearly not Emily's forte.

Sylvia Rosenberg came out of the kitchen, where she had been chattering with Emily, and embraced Jessup. "Do you know how long it's been!" she exclaimed. "We haven't seen you since you left for India!" "I know!" smiled Jessup. Introductions were made. "Sylvia, this is Mason Parrish—" "It's been more than seven years since we've seen these two people!" cried Sylvia. Parrish beamed through his beard. Jessup plunked himself down on one of the torn overstuffed chairs in the living room, Margaret instantly asleep on his chest. "Emily's an associate professor now, you know," he informed Rosenberg, who was lounging on the sofa.

"Yeah, I know; she told me," said Rosenberg. "You guys must be loaded, two professors in the family."

"We've got a summer place in Maine. You guys can use it, if you'd like. Emily's going to Africa; I'll be in Mexico this summer. Listen, do you know a guy named Echeverría, University of Mexico, says he worked with you at Langley Porter?"

"Sure. Very bright guy."

"Well, he's here in Boston at the Botanical Museum. We'll all have to get together. I'm going back to Mexico with him in June."

"What're you going to do in Mexico?"

"Well, Echeverría's got this witch doctor down there, the Hinchi Indians, did you ever hear of the Hinchi Indians? They're an isolated tribe in central Mexico, near San Luis Potosí, who still practice the ancient Toltec rituals, sacred mushroom ceremonies, that sort of thing. Apparently, they use some kind of hallucinatory compound that's supposed to evoke a common experience for all users, interesting if true."

Rosenberg sighed. "You're still screwing around with altered consciousness, I see."

"Oh, yeah."

"Ever get into an isolation tank anymore?"

"No. It's a little out of fashion, I think. They've got one here at the medical school, but I don't think anybody's used it in five or six years, not since the sixties. How about you?"

"No."

Emily came in from the kitchen. "My God, Arthur, I forgot to ask you—do you want any coffee, cookies? We've got all kinds of junk food around for the kids."

"Terrific," said Rosenberg.

"How about you, Mason?"

Parrish was lying on the floor flat on his back, pretending to have been knocked out cold by five-year-old Grace, who was giggling with glee.

Jessup stood. "Listen, I better put this one in her bed."

He carried the sleeping Margaret into her bedroom. Rosenberg followed him, lounged in the doorway, watched as Jessup laid the child in her bed and covered her with a blanket. The room was dark and, it seemed to Rosenberg, considerably messier than most kids' rooms. There were opened cardboard cartons here and there and little dresses, still on their hangers, lying on the other bed, toys piled in haphazard heaps. Nevertheless, it was affecting to see Jessup's tender concern for his daughter.

"You and Emily seem to have made a good go of it, Eddie," he said.

Jessup looked up at him from the shadows on the other side of the bed, smiled. "You're kidding, aren't you? We're splitting up. Emily and I are separating. I took for granted Emily had already told you."

"What do you mean, you're splitting up?"

"I mean, Emily and the kids are moving out. She's found a house in Cambridge for next year, and they're letting her store her stuff. My God, Arthur, you don't think we live in this sort of disorder all the time? Emily's a lousy housekeeper, but she isn't this bad."

Rosenberg was genuinely startled. "I don't believe this!" he snorted. "We haven't seen you people in seven years, and the first thing we find out is she's going to Africa in three weeks, and you're going to Mexico in June, and now you're telling me you're splitting up altogether! What about all those happy letters you wrote us, how everything was so terrific?"

"Emily wrote the letters, Arthur. And she lied. Or perhaps she thought she was happy at the time. The kids have been a great source of pleasure to her. And her work has been going well. I suppose, with a little self-deception, she might have thought herself happy. And I tried, Arthur. I'm not a complete son of a bitch. I'm not cruel. I did try to put on a good show of being a good husband and a good father. But that's what it was, a show. There wasn't an ounce of truth in it."

He regarded his child's sleeping form on the shadowed bed with what seemed a tender expression. He looked up at Rosenberg again, his eyes suddenly white in the grayness of the room. "It's all shit," he murmured, "it's all artifice." He came around the bed and stopped again, frowned at the floor. "I pretend to be a doting father. It's not real. I don't feel anything real right now for this kid except relief perhaps that she's finally asleep. Oh, I do it all. I'm an attentive father, a concerned father. I take them to the zoo, I tickle their stomachs. I sit with them when they're ill, romp with them when they're well, hold them when they're frightened. I'm even stern sometimes. I even enjoy them now and then.

But I can't help it, Arthur. Mostly, I want to be rid of them. I want to be alone. I have a great deal of unfinished business with myself. I need to confront myself. Because the self I have at the moment is a very shoddy, makeshift thing, contrived, illusory, unreal, lacking truth and substance, constantly pretending, constantly lying, shifting, taking different forms. I want to find a true self, an immutable self. I want to get down to the embedded rock of life, what Saint John would call the bare and barren soul. It's me that wants the divorce, Arthur, not Emily. She's quite content to go on the way we are. She insists she's in love with me, whatever that is. What she really means is she prefers this arbitrary structure we've created to being alone. She prefers the senseless pain we inflict on each other to the pain we would otherwise inflict on ourselves. But I'm not afraid of that solitary pain. I'm like one of the early patristic anchorites. I want to go off into the desert like Saint Anthony. If I can't find God, I at least want to find my self."

Jessup came out of the grayness of the room into the thin spill of daylight at the doorway. He was honestly fond of Rosenberg. He rested his hand on Rosenberg's shoulder and said, "Why don't I call Echeverría and we'll go out and have dinner?"

"Terrific!" said Rosenberg.

They went to Dom's and made a noisy, cheerful table, eight voluble academics, all in their mid-thirties, gabbling simultaneously about their work, stowing their pasta away, swilling their wine. Emily was telling Parrish's girl for the night, a second-year medical student from Mass General, that she was going to Africa to study baboon vocalizations.

("What differentiates man from the chimpanzee, for example, is the fact that man needs tools for survival and therefore evolved a cortical structure that could make use of tools. A chimpanzee might use a stick to dig into a termite hill, but he can survive as a species without it. A baboon, whose diet is almost exclusively vegetarian, will take half an hour to dig up a root. It just has never occurred to baboons they could shorten that time to five minutes if they used a stick. Originally, man was just another savanna-living primate like the baboon. All right, what were the specific survival conditions existing on the savannas of East and South Africa that forced one specific group of apes to begin using a stick to dig up their food? Presumably, there must have been some common mechanism to both baboons and emergent man. . . .")

Parrish was flirting with Echeverría's girl, a botanist from the Botanical Museum. ("Nobody really knows how memory works. Apparently, we remember everything we sense for about fifty milliseconds; then it disappears or is selectively fixed in our consciousness. Now you being a botanist, sure as hell got to know puromycin can wipe out a memory, and sympathomimetic drugs like strychnine, dextroamphetamine, et cetera, can stimulate the retention of a memory. But these are all poisonous, addictive, induce convulsions and are alien to the body. The fact that a small chain of amino acids, $ACTH^{4-7}$, a natural substance of the body, is instrumental in fixing memory is, I think, particularly interesting. This, however, raises another question. ACTH is a peptide. Its secretory rates are influenced by stress. Does ACTH actually code learning or does it only relate to hormonal substances that formed due to stress? You really interested in this shit, honey? Because if you are, I'll be glad to go to considerable lengths any night this week . . .")

Rosenberg was ranging around the dinner table trying to get everyone to sign a petition demanding that the NIH guidelines on recombinant DNA research be reviewed and made stricter. "For Pete's sake," Emily paused in her own chattering to comment. "You haven't been in Boston four days, Arthur, and you're already a member of the Committee of Concerned Scientists." She signed nevertheless. Rosenberg, who had always been a radical scientist, was also a member of Science for the People, the Committee for Morality in Science, and the Boston Area Recombinant DNA Group. The Asilomar Conference had met just two months before and had established some rules for recombinant DNA research, moderate and high-risk labs, and even failsafe biological protections. These regulations were considered insufficient by many radical scientists, who were now calling for even more stringent rules to be set down by the NIH. This was the substance of Rosenberg's petition, and he squeezed in beside Echeverría to persuade him to sign. ("We scientists have a moral obligation to the public as well as to our own research. Some of those shotgun fragments could augment a bacterium's ability to produce disease. For God's sake, they're chopping up fruit flies and inserting the segments into E coli and mass-producing the bacteria. We're dealing with a fistful of unknowns. We can only identify a couple of the genes. And now there's a lot of talk about sticking a P–3 lab here in Cambridge. They've already got them at Stanford and the U of M, and the whole thing with tumor viruses is already out of hand at Woods Hole. I mean, we could wipe out the planet if we don't watch out, so just sign the damn thing, Eduardo. . . .")

And Jessup, who had had more wine than was his wont, was loudly explaining the Buddhist concept of self to Sylvia Rosenberg and to anybody else whose attention he could grab.

"As a matter of fact," he announced to Sylvia, "the whole yogic experience was a little disappointing. No matter how you slice it, it's still a state-specific technology operating in the service of an a priori belief system, not much different from other trance-inducing techniques. The breathing exercises are effective as hell. The breathing becomes an entity in itself, an actual state of consciousness in its own right, so that your body breathing becomes the embodiment of your breath. But it's still a renunciatory technique to achieve a predetermined trancelike state, what the Zen people call an isness, a very pure narcissism, Freud's oceanic feeling. What dignifies the yogic practices is that the belief system itself is not truly religious. There is no Buddhist god per se. It is the Self, the individual Mind, that contains immortality and ultimate truth—"

"What the hell's not metaphysical about that?" shouted Emily from her end of the table, interrupting her own colloquy. "You've simply replaced God with the Original Self."

"Yes, but we've localized it, haven't we!" Jessup shouted back. "At least we know where the Self is! It's in our own minds, somewhere in those hundred-odd billion neural and glial cells in our own minds! It's a form of human energy! If there is an Original Consciousness or a Jungian consciousness or whatever the hell you want to call it, it took in a lot of sensory input, and that input is stored away somewhere in our minds in the quantifiable form of memory! Memory is energy! It doesn't disappear! It's still in there!" He was on his feet now, staggering a little, not really able to hold four flagons of red wine. He wheeled to Rosenberg. "I'm telling you there's a physiological pathway to our earlier consciousnesses! And I'm telling you it's somewhere in the goddamned limbic system! If I could stick a couple of microelectrodes into your skull, I'll bet my last shirt we would revive long-term memory and even prenatal recall, and if that isn't a prior consciousness, I'll eat my hat!"

"Jessup, you are a whacko!" roared Parrish happily.

Jessup, who had wandered some steps away from his seat, found his way back, sat down, poured himself another glass of wine. One of those inexplicable hushes had descended on the gathering, out of which Jessup's abruptly quiet, contemplative voice could be clearly heard. "What's whacko about it, Mason?" he asked agreeably. "I'm a man in search of his true self. How archetypically American can you get? Everybody's looking for his true self. We're all trying to fulfill ourselves, understand ourselves, get in touch with ourselves, get ahold of ourselves, face the reality of ourselves, explore ourselves, expand ourselves. Ever since we dispensed with God, we've got nothing but ourselves to explain this meaningless horror of life. We're all weekending at est or meditating for forty minutes a day or squatting on floors in a communal OM or locking arms in quasi-Sufi dances or stripping off the deceptions of civilized life and jumping naked into a swimming pool filled with other naked searchers for self. Well, I think that true self, that original self, that first self, is a real, mensurate, quantifiable thing, tangible and incarnate. And I'm going to find the fucker."

Zapatecus, Mexico

June 1975

Actually, the Hinchi Indians weren't in San Luis Potosí but in Zapatecus Province, a tribe of pre-Aztecs living amid the brutal barrancas of central Mexico. They were descendants of the Chichimec Toltecs, but the local *brujo* turned out to be a Tarahumara Indian who had married into the tribe. That helped because he spoke a little Spanish; the others none at all. Echeverría served as interpreter. He and Jessup joined the Hinchis just as they set off on their long trek to the sacred mushroom fields, an expedition lasting three weeks, the whole tribe of some eight hundred, in their loincloths and cotton shirts, loping along through the violently colored valleys and shocking gorges, pausing every other night to get drunk on corn beer. It was fetching country, filled with blue agave and yellow chaparral, and the crags in the unapproachable distances were splashed orange by the relentless summer sun.

The *brujo* was a good-hearted soul in his late sixties, whose earlier contact with white civilization was affirmed by the shapeless gray single-breasted jacket he wore, the white tails of his loincloth hanging down from beneath it like the fringes of a prayer shawl. The Hinchis, he explained to Echeverría and Jessup, retained only a little of their original animistic religion, at most a nodding acknowledgment to the feathered serpent god, Quetzalcoatl. They had somehow evolved their own code of beliefs based on spiritual and life-giving forces. Jessup thought that curiously Oriental. At any rate, the tribe filled a number of burlap bags with mushrooms, branches of small slender trees, leaves, petals, seed pods, and white, tuberous roots, moving across the sacred plateau like cotton pickers, sometimes going to their knees to scrape out the roots with their hands. Jessup in Levi's and T-shirt stood on the fringe of the activity with his Sony tape recorder while Echeverría, who was a botanist, explained that the plants were sinicuiche or hema salicifolia, and the mushrooms were almost certainly amanita muscaria, "a very powerful psychedelic, and a little dangerous. It contains some belladonna alkaloids, atropine, scopolamine. The sinicuiche plant is highly regarded among a number of Indian tribes. I've seen it as far north as Chihuahua. It should be especially interesting for you. The Indians say it invokes old memories, even ancient ones. The Hinchis call it the First Flower."

"First in the sense of primordial?"

"Yes, in the sense of the Most Ancient."

"I'd like to try it," said Jessup. "Do you think they'll let me join their smoking ritual?"

"They seem like agreeable people," said Echeverría.

They all got back to their home valley on the twelfth of July. Most of the tribe went on a *tesgüinada*, a two-day binge of corn beer, while a number of chosen women ground the various roots and buds and leaves and petals into varying degrees of fineness. The separate powders and crumbled mushrooms were stored away for a year in sealed gourds to become sufficiently moldy. Then last year's gourds were brought out, and the preparations for the smoking ritual begun. Only five men, *los escogidos*, actually participated. The old *brujo* was, of course, one. The ceremony took place in front of the *brujo's* house, a ramshackle clapboard shanty with a shaky overhang held up by two rotting planks. They got a fire going and sprawled around it. Three large stones formed the hearth. The *brujo* came out of his shack with a burlap bag, which he emptied item by item. The first was a hunting knife, nearly a foot in length and glistening blue in the late afternoon sunlight. Then a soft brown leather pouch, then a brown leather sheath, pitted and verdigrised with age, from which he extracted the ceremonial pipe, a dark-reddish stem about ten inches long with a blackened bowl. He spaced them carefully on the blanket and bowed to each of the four directions, chanting in a low whine. Then he reached into the bag and removed the last item, a bundle of bound white plant roots, from which he drew one out and split it down the middle with his knife till it formed a Y. He paused in his humming chant to mutter some Spanish to Echeverría, who, in turn, leaned across to Jessup and said, "He wants to know if you still want to participate."

"Yes, of course," said Jessup.

The old *brujo* went back to his soft chant. One of the women brought out a large pot and set it on the stones over the fire. Jessup leaned over to see what was in it. It was a quarter-filled with a sludgelike yellow substance. The *brujo* explained it was boiled mushroom caps, *los bonguitos*, which had been calcining for two days now, since the return from the sacred fields. He resumed his chanting, all the while binding together the forked ends of the root with what seemed to be the tendrils of a vine. At Jessup's request, Echeverría asked the old man, "What sort of experience can my friend expect?"

The old man, without pausing in his binding, said, "His soul will return to his First Soul."

Echeverría translated the answer. Jessup, who had been watching the reels on the tape recorder cassette slowly turn, looked up sharply. "Did he use those words exactly?"

"Yes," said Echeverría.

"That's practically Buddhist," murmured Jessup, and replaced the used cassette in the recording machine with a fresh one. When the machine was started again, he asked Echeverría to ask the old man: "What does the First Soul look like?"

Echeverría translated. The old *brujo* answered. Echeverría translated. "It is Unborn Stuff."

Jessup stared at the *brujo*, who now, apparently finished with preparing the root, turned to regard Jessup.

The last of the sun had just disappeared behind the distant peaks, and their little valley was abruptly in heavy shadow. Jessup couldn't make out the old man's features, not five feet away from him, but he could see the eyes, which seemed to be glowing preternaturally, like those of a jungle cat. The *brujo* addressed an uncharacteristically long speech to Jessup, six sentences in Spanish, waiting at the end of each for Echeverría to translate.

"You will be sick," the old man told Jessup. "Then you will shoot into void. You will see a spot. The spot will become a streak. This is the Crack Between the Nothing. Out of this Nothing will come your Unborn Soul."

Jessup nodded. It was too good to be true. He might have been talking to a Tibetan yogi.

The old *brujo* muttered something in Spanish to Echeverría, who told Jessup: "He wants you to hold the root. Put out your hand palm up."

Jessup edged closer and stuck out his hand. The *brujo* carefully placed the root across the flat of his palm, and then, suddenly, he separated Jessup's third and fourth fingers and deftly slashed the flesh with his hunting knife. Jessup, who had read Castaneda, should have expected something like this, but he didn't, and he screamed into the gathering stillness of the twilight as he felt the blood stream from the cut. So petrified was he by the suddenness of it that he left his hand outstretched, palm open. The *brujo* seized his wrist and pulled his bleeding hand over the pot. He twisted Jessup's wrist so that the stark white root fell into the pot, and he held Jessup's hand there till a few drops of blood joined the caking calx below. The old man released him, and he fell onto the ground, shocked and utterly spent, sick with a sense of outrage.

"Are you all right?" asked Echeverría.

Jessup nodded.

The old *brujo* and one of the other men were now lifting the pot off the hearthstones and moving it to the ritual blanket. To Jessup, lying in the sudden night, they seemed like monstrous shadows. He tried to study his damaged hand in the darkness. The bleeding seemed to have stopped. "Jesus Christ," he muttered. He was startled by a form looming over him. It was the *brujo*, holding out the pipe to him expressionlessly. Jessup sat up, accepted the pipe and began to smoke it.

He was immediately seized with nausea and began to vomit onto the ground. None of the other men paid any attention. The old *brujo* was asking Echeverría if the recording machine was on. When informed that it was, he began to explain in Spanish that the mixture Jessup was smoking contained three parts of the dried mushroom calx in the pot to one part sinicuiche powder and one part the powder of some third plant with a Toltec name which Echeverría tried to repeat but couldn't. All this Jessup heard clearly as he bent over on one elbow and retched. The nausea disappeared instantly; the retching had been smooth and painless. Then, abruptly, he was propelled upward into instant hallucination. The little clearing in which he had been squatting disappeared beneath him, or rather disappeared to the size of a pinpoint miles below, which slowly attenuated till it took on the form of a slit, a jagged slit, a crack. This Jessup took to be the Crack Between the Nothing. Then slowly the slit of light began to enfold out of itself in flowing surflike emanations of light, so blinding that Jessup imagined he was in the presence of some original illumination. This effusion of light expanded and lapped out of itself in enormous, inexorable waves until Jessup was encompassed entirely within it and was a brilliant white spot himself. Effulgent whiteness stretched from horizon to horizon in an incessantly expanding, horizonless space, an infinity. A column of halos rose out of the whiteness, annulated like the trunk of a tree, evolving into a golden helix, involuting around itself and filled with frantic, vermiform, fork-shaped spots of pulsating light like a microscopic view of holy chromosomes. He heard a high-pitched scream of exultancy, which was odd because psychedelic hallucinations rarely invoke auditory responses.

Suddenly, there emerged from the original pinspot of light, which was now stark black, a brownish figure, if it could be called a figure, more a molten mass of substance which appeared to have arms and legs and a head, but so protean of form that the limbs and other distinguishing features kept dissolving into itself and extruding out of itself, bubbling up here and there, swelling and contracting. As it emerged larger and larger, the substance seemed to be iridescent, sparkling, flaring with tiny flames that proved on closer examination to be exploding neural matter. This thing became huger and huger, and its color became redder and redder and then increasingly golden. Jessup abruptly recalled that gold is the color for the archaic age in the yogic cycle, and red the color of the magic age. He witnessed this extraordinary image with no fear; if anything, he watched

with awe as it approached him. Then, suddenly, a large lizard, colored exuberantly yellow (the color of the mythic
age), flitted across the white expanse and was engulfed by
the flaming molten substance, ripped with a sickening
scream of bone and muscle, and devoured. The scene, which
would have revolted Jessup in real life, he now watched
with a benign smile. Having paused for its meal, the mass of
substance now continued to Jessup and engulfed him,
painlessly and gently. He felt infused with endless power.
Engulfed in the substance, he catapulted himself into
infinity. It was the most exhilarating moment of his life.

The hallucinatory part of the experience lasted about
an hour. The descent was precipitous and made him a little
ill. He was startled to find he was standing in a small bosk of
bushes. His hands were scratched as if by the brambles. The
other men were still sitting around their fire about thirty
yards away, taking little puffs from the ceremonial pipe or
biting peyote buttons. It was full night now. His watch,
when he looked at it near the fire a few moments later,
showed 8:19. He rejoined the others, squatted down beside
his tape recorder and just stared at the flames. In a few minutes, he was fast asleep.

The next day, the *brujo* asked him if he had had the experience that had been predicted for him. Jessup nodded,
then added that he had an experience that had not been
predicted for him. The shaman nodded and said, "You ate a
lizard."

Jessup was a little startled by this, but pleased. "How
do you know I ate a lizard?" he asked.

Echeverría interpreted. The *brujo* regarded him blankly.

"Because I saw you eat the lizard," he said. "We all saw you eat the lizard."

Jessup considered this for a moment and then asked through Echeverría: "Does that mean you were with me in my dream? That you have the ability to get into another man's dream?"

The old *brujo* scowled, perhaps a little confused. The Hinchi Indians, like small children, don't see a sharp difference between dreams and external reality. The shaman repeated: "I saw you eat the lizard. We all saw you."

Jessup persisted: "But I ate the lizard in my dream. I didn't eat the lizard here around the fire. If you saw me eat the lizard, you must have been with me in my dream."

Echeverría translated this into Spanish. The *brujo* didn't seem to understand. Echeverría rephrased it into more elementary Spanish. The *brujo* scowled at Jessup and then shuffled off toward the bushes where Jessup had returned from his hallucination. He turned back after a few steps and clearly wanted Jessup to come after him. Jessup and Echeverría followed. The *brujo* brushed his way into the bushes and paused and pointed down at the ground. What Jessup and Echeverría saw was the half-eaten remains of a large spine-crested iguana lizard, whose limbs had been wrenched out of their sockets. Echeverría was sick on the spot.

The *brujo* walked away and wouldn't talk anymore about it. He seemed, in fact, offended. Within the hour, of course, Jessup was regarding the matter with complete skepticism. First of all, you don't find iguanas in the highlands; they are desert and shore creatures. It was a trick the In-

dians had played on him just to make the gringo look a fool.
The lizard had been thrown to the several dogs that were
constantly hanging about and devoured by them. Not that
dogs are known to wrench the limbs off their prey, but the
Indians might have done that. He plagued Echeverría about
the events of the preceding night. Echeverría had not participated in the ceremony and had presumably been a sober
observer. Echeverría's answers were not entirely reassuring.
Echeverría said that at around seven-thirty the night before, Jessup had got up and gone off into the bushes, presumably to urinate. He had been gone for at least twenty minutes, during which time there had been a short explosion of
animal noises, snarls and growls and screams. It had
sounded a little like two dogs fighting with each other.
Echeverría and one of the women had got up to see what
had happened, thinking a couple of the dogs might have set
on Jessup or that Jessup might have had some ill effects
from the mushroom-smoking. It had, after all, been the first
time he had ever tried any hallucinogen, and you never
know about first times. In any event, Echeverría and the
woman had just about reached the edge of the boscage
when the snarling and screaming stopped, and the *brujo*
called to them to come back. Which they did.

"For God's sake!" snapped Jessup. "You're not even en-
tertaining the possibility that I went off into those bushes,
captured myself an enormous iguana lizard, tore it limb from
limb and devoured it!"

"Of course not," said Echeverría.

"And in twenty goddam minutes!" said Jessup.

"I'm only telling you what happened, that's all," said Echeverría.

"Hallucinations don't externalize," said Jessup. "As far as you know, I retained my normal shape and form and sat around the fire like the others. I didn't turn into a molten mass of neural substance, did I?"

"No, no," Echeverría reassured him. "You didn't change shape. That was purely hallucinatory. You went off for twenty minutes to take a piss and came back. Later you wandered around a bit here in the clearing. You stood over there for a while. Then you came back, sat down and went to sleep. That was around eight."

"Okay," said Jessup. "Sorry I got fractious. Listen, do you think they'd let me take some of that mixture back to Boston with me?"

Boston: Harvard Medical School, Peter Bent Brigham Hospital

October 1975—January 1976

Mason Millard Parrish, thirty-seven years old, six foot two, lumbering and bearded, professor of endocrinology at the Harvard School of Medicine, attending endocrinologist on the staff of the Peter Bent Brigham Hospital, consulting editor of the *American Journal of Endocrinology,* director of clinical research of the New England Endocrinological Society, didn't participate in Jessup's curious experiments until late in October 1975. It was not that he was unaware of the activities of his friends, Rosenberg and Jessup. He knew Rosenberg had synthesized the hallucinogenic mixture Jessup had brought back from Mexico and that they were doing some ad hoc investigation of the stuff. But he hadn't seen very much of his friends; he was a very busy man. He had his own research, of course. He had started off six years before, trying to track down the function of ACTH in the fixing of short-term memory, and the project had since expanded into a sizable enterprise with a big grant from the NIH. He had a large lab now, with five cages full of scampering rats, two lab technicians, two grad students, an endocrinology fellow and a full-time secretary. He did attending rounds three mornings a week. He was the administrator of the weekly faculty endocrine conferences (Tuesdays at 11 A.M.), he presided over the Journal Club (Fridays at 4 P.M.), and he did clinic and outpatient work on Tuesday afternoons and Thursday mornings; and he taught: two classes. A bachelor, he was something of a swinger, an exuberant fellow who raced around Boston on a Honda and regularly fell in love. On Friday, October 17, he was not in love and didn't have a date, so he called Rosenberg to see what he was up to. Rosenberg said Jessup was going to take another ride on his Mexican drug that night; they were going to be in one of the sound-attenuated rooms up at the Psychophysiology Department at the Brigham around seven o'clock.

"Why don't I drop over and bullshit a little?" said Parrish.

"Terrific," said Rosenberg.

At seven o'clock that evening, Parrish was roaming the fourth floor of the Brigham, poking his head into the biofeedback rooms, looking for his friends. He found them in the last of the rooms, a small chamber lined with porous soundproofing tiles and containing only a large relaxing chair, on which Jessup was reclining, and a portable set of electroencephalographic equipment. The lighting was subdued. A large glass window separated the room from the monitor room. Jessup held a large porcelain basin in his lap.

"What's that for?" asked Parrish.

"There's a lot of vomiting goes on with this," said Jessup.

Rosenberg handed Jessup a kitchen glass with a clear liquid in it, which Jessup drank. Rosenberg set to work applying the EEG leads to Jessup's scalp.

"What're you guys doing anyway?" said Parrish.

"Well, like I told you, Mason," said Rosenberg, "we've got a real pisser here. This is a ten-milligram-per-cc solution. We've been taking it in hundred-milligram doses, but the last couple of times we've upped it to two hundred, and let me tell you, it'll give you a hell of a ride. You hallucinate like a son of a bitch. You want to take a shot at it sometime?"

"Shit, no. I stopped biting peyote buttons back in my sophomore year."

"Well, this is no peyote button. We're getting some pretty curious readings. We've been picking up a metabolite on the order of adenochrome or taraxeine in both our urines. That's the metabolite Heath found when they were working on schizophrenics. Who knows, maybe we can blow Snyder and his dopamine people right off the map."

"Mason," said Jessup, "we're picking up things that should be right up your alley. We're picking up abnormally excessive levels of VMA and HIAA and seventeen-hydroxy-and-keto-steroids."

"Jesus," said Parrish. "What the hell are your adrenals up to? How long have you been getting values like this?"

"Take it easy, Mason," said Jessup. "All the baseline and follow-up values are normal."

"You haven't been symptomatic?"

"Nothing. Everything's fine. Really." Jessup drained the kitchen glass.

"What's in that shit you're drinking anyway?"

"Two hundred milligrams of this stuff isn't going to hurt anybody," said Rosenberg. "Hallucinogens wash out in less than twenty-four hours anyway." He led Parrish back into the monitor room, closing the door after them. He clicked the mike on. "How're you doing?" he murmured into the mike.

Jessup's voice came back: "Fine."

Rosenberg, perched on his stool, looking like a Talmudic student, folded his hands between his knees, frowned, pursed his lips, and said, "What's going to happen, Mason, is he'll start to throw up in a couple of minutes, and then, about five, ten minutes after that, he'll take off."

He glanced through the glass window, and indeed, Jessup had begun to retch into the porcelain basin on his lap, the green bile issuing effortlessly and with no visible pain. "What's weird about this compound," Rosenberg continued, "are the hallucinations. They're repeatable. I've never run across a psychoactive substance that produces repeatable hallucinations. I've taken the stuff myself three times, and not only are my hallucinations the same each time, but they're much the same as Eddie's. It's real weird. We've been working on the two-hundred-milligram level the last four times—I took it once, Eddie took it three times—and what happens is you suddenly shoot up into a void, just nothing everywhere, a big white nothing. Then a crack appears, and out of the crack comes a cell-like structure. It's got a membrane and a nuclear structure in the middle that's boiling like the molten core of the earth. Jessup calls it the incarnated id, our original nuclear self, boiling with our most primal hungers. And this id comes at you on fire, an inferno, flaming up like the sun. Telling it to you now, it sounds a little scary, but in the hallucination you get a terrific beatific feeling. Eddie keeps all the tapes of these trips in his office. You ought to listen to them—"

Somebody from the Psychophysiology Department opened the door and leaned in. "Wischenschaft said we could use the room," said Rosenberg. The intruder left.

"What's in that stuff you're drinking?" asked Parrish.

"Nothing special. A lot of alkaloids, principally cryogenine, some harmine, some harmaline. The bulk of it is from the amanita muscaria mushroom, which is muscimol, ibotanic acid, muscazon, the belladonna alkaloids, some muscarine, N-dimethyl-five-hydroxytryptomine and some acetylcholine."

"You may be getting close to toxic levels with two hundred milligrams."

"Oh, we're not going to take more than two hundred—are you kidding? Eddie's idea is to try this all out using the isolation tank in B Building. Because you get a surprising lot of external interference in these biofeedback rooms. You keep seeing your own reflection in that window. It's an impure set of conditions, really. So Eddie wants to try two hundred milligrams of this stuff in the isolation tank, where external stimuli are wiped out altogether." He leaned over to study the EEG readings. "Look at that, Mason. He went into theta like a shot. Less than a minute. No spindling, nothing. We've had these EEG readings every time, both of us. Eddie's convinced this compound goes straight to the limbic system, which would be pretty weird, because I never saw a psychoactive that didn't wind up in the liver or the kidney."

"Man, why don't you just shoot up a couple of rats and retrieve the stuff?"

"We were going to ask you tonight if we could use your lab."

"Hell, yeah, you can use my lab. I'll let you have a couple of rats. If you want to fractionate the stuff, I'll take you down to Charlie Shimona's lab. Do you know Charlie?"

"No."

"He's got all kinds of room down there."

Jessup's voice suddenly announced over the intercom: "Okay, here I go; you can start the tape."

Rosenberg pressed the start button on the Sony recorder and murmured into it: "Friday, October seventeen, nineteen seventy-five, seven twenty-six P.M."

The reels of the cassette slowly turned. Jessup's voice began to issue out of the intercom.

"Okay, I'm going up now . . . lots of interference. I'm picking up smells. I can smell the hospital . . . I'm picking up reflections off the window. Some spatial distortion. My reflection seems to be about a hundred yards away. I'm getting interim imagery now, an avenue of menhirs, a cromlech

of megaliths, a thumb-sized thole, a blastula with a fur-
rowed fetal caul. . . . Okay, I'm free and clear. I'm up there.
Total void, horizon to horizon, a timeless scour of white. I
think all that interim hallucinating is time-linked. All the
imagery is antique past, paleolithic. Old, old stones; it's always old, old stones. Remind me to start boning up on some
geology. I'm convinced the early imagery is time-linked.
Okay, texture changing, heavy impasto quality, laid on with
a big brush, streaky, bubbling, the usual. . . ."

A pause. Parrish stared, curiously disturbed, at the
scrawling fingers of the polygraph machine.

Jessup's disembodied voice began again, intoning into
the compressed monitor room: "The crack, the crack, forming now—have you ever noticed the crack forms by an in-
folding like the first development of a fetal neural
tube? . . . Okay, negative reversal, it's all endless black,
endless space black. The crack is a molten line, boiling like a
volcano, widening at the tip, usual pattern, integumentation, boiling blue nuclear structure, the usual mini-astro-
nomical explosions going on, whirling matter shooting off
everywhere, the birth of a star, whatever the hell it is, here
it comes, here it comes. . . ."

"Here what comes?" muttered Parrish.

"The cell-like structure has exploded off its mooring
and comes sailing out at you," explained Rosenberg.

"What happens then?"

"It eats you."

"What do you mean, it eats you?"

"It comes right at you, engulfs you like a paramecium,

ingests you, and you get digested into the boiling blue nucleus."

"Man, that's weird."

"As a matter of fact, it's very serene."

Jessup's voice: "I'm in the id, I'm in the id. . . ."

The room was strangely, suddenly silent, except, after a moment, for the slow whirring of the reels of the tape recorder's cassette. Rosenberg sat perched on his stool, his eyes closed, his hands clasped between his knees. After a long moment, he said, "That's it."

"What do you mean, that's it?" said Parrish. "What happens after you get into the id?"

"You fall asleep," said Rosenberg. "That's as far as any of the tapes go. I've been into the id three times, and I don't remember a damn thing. All the tapes, even Eddie's, stop here."

They sat in silence for a moment. Through the window they could see Jessup leaning back on his chair, rigid, entranced, in the diffuse shadows of the soundproofed room.

"How long does this go on?" muttered Parrish.

"Twenty minutes, half an hour."

"Sure waste a lot of tape."

"And a hell of a lot of polygraph paper. We've used about four hundred bucks' worth already. Eddie's been pinching the money out of his grant."

"And that's it?"

"That's it."

"What happens after he comes off his high?"

"Nothing. We go get a hamburger."

"Jesus, you guys are like two kids dropping acid in the dorm."

"You ought to try it one time. It'll give you a real weird ride."

"No, thanks."

They fell into silence. Parrish's cigar had gone out. He relit it, puffed, stretched his long legs out, closed his eyes. The reels of the cassette revolved slowly.

"Look at that," said Rosenberg suddenly.

Parrish opened his eyes. Rosenberg was standing at the window, staring into the soundproofed room. Parrish half rose to see what was happening. Jessup was still lying in what seemed to be an immobilized trance, his head back against the cushioned leather of the chair, his eyes closed, but his face was contorting into fierce grimaces, his mouth opening into silent strangulated rictus, as if he was trying to say something desperately necessary but couldn't get the words out. Then his voice exploded over the intercom in a blare.

"Pitted cratered caldera-ed blazing hot moon terrain," he croaked.

Rosenberg clicked the intercom. "Are you okay, Eddie?"

"I'm fine!" shouted Jessup's voice. "Get this stuff! This is new! Twin cones of volcanic craters like owl eyes! Way back, volcanic activity! Phlegethon! Ancient river of fire! Pyroclastic debris, lapilli! Large shallow marshy basin! Geosyncline. My God! It's cracking, it's cracking, the whole thing is cracking! Enormous mosses of rock rising up in shafts, deafening! The noise is deafening! Can you hear me! An agonizing wrenching of rock! A fucking mountain is raging up from the bottomless pit! The most unbelievable fucking thing I've ever seen! Fifty-ton rocks are rising out of the sea, massive earth crust, white-hot rocks, steaming, fracturing, folding over each other! I'm watching the birth agony of a mountain! My God, can't you hear it! The whole damn thing! As far as the eye can see! An endless, cracking rupture of rock and mantle! A hundred feet high and huge and keeps piling! And the sun became black as sackcloth, the full moon became like blood, and a great mountain, burning with fire, was thrown into the sea, and the beast ascends from the bottomless pit, and the angel of the bottomless pit, his name in Hebrew is Abaddon!"

Then, an abrupt silence. Through the window they could see that Jessup's face was serene again.

Rosenberg clicked the intercom. "Are you okay, Eddie?" he murmured into the mike.

"I'm fine," came Jessup's startlingly soft, calm, disembodied voice.

"Do you want me to bring you down?"

"I feel just fine, really."

"Okay," said Rosenberg. He clicked off, turned to Parrish. "Monday afternoon okay?"

"What about Monday afternoon?"

"I'd like to bring some of this compound over, see if we can localize the stuff."

"Monday'll be fine."

On Monday afternoon, Parrish and Rosenberg took three rats out of their cage, injected them with seven milligrams/kilograms of the compound, which had been labeled with tritium to make it traceable. An hour later, they sliced off the rats' heads in the guillotine box. The heads and the bodies were then autopsied, the organs harvested and ground up, and an aliquot of each organ separately inserted into the scintillation counter. When they put in the brain, the counter began ticking actively.

"Son of a bitch," muttered Parrish. "He was right—it's all in the brain."

"I bet you we retrieved at least half that compound," said Rosenberg.

"More," said Parrish. "Man, we've got something weird here."

On Wednesday, they confirmed the results with histofluorescent techniques. On this occasion, Jessup, who didn't teach on Wednesdays, joined them. They shot up three more rats, chopped off their heads, extracted their organs, sliced them into microtomal sections, applied regular and fluorescent antibodies, and examined each slice under an ultraviolet microscope. The fluorescing antigen-antibody complexes were visible as gleaming little dots. The compound had clearly localized in the limbic system. The hippocampal gyrus was loaded with the stuff. "Unless I'm out of my gourd," said Parrish, "they're in the nerve cell body."

"Hell," said Jessup, "inside the goddam nucleus."

"I've got to fractionate this stuff," said Rosenberg.

On Monday, October 27, 1975, Parrish and Rosenberg brought three trays of rats' organs down to Charles Shimona's biochemistry lab, where, discouraging Shimona's amiable Oriental curiosity, they homogenized the organs in a blender and stuck the mess into a centrifuge at 2000 revs/sec. After twenty minutes, they took out the layer of heavier nuclei that had sedimented and examined the homogenate. Some 70 percent of the compound was eventually retrieved, and some 80 percent of that was found in the heavy nuclei.

"I'll bet you this fucker's in the chromosomes," muttered Parrish.

They put an aliquot of the solution into the chromotography column and poured solvent in and let it filter down. Jessup joined them three hours later, when he had finished his afternoon class. Parrish and Rosenberg were just taking the filtrate out and pouring it into a liquid scintillation spectrometer which they had programmed for the constituents of the compound. It matched. They again retrieved an overwhelming proportion of the drug, and most of what was retrieved was in the nuclei.

"You ever know a psychoactive drug to act on a nuclear level?" mumbled Parrish.

"Nope," said Rosenberg. "They alter membranes or synapses or block receptor sites."

"Only antimetabolites work on a nuclear level."

"I'd like to see if it binds to nucleic acids," said Jessup.

"Well, we better sign up for it now," said Parrish, "because the last time I used x-ray crystallography, I had to stand on line for two weeks."

Parrish was, of course, caught up in the inquiry by now. In fact, it was really bugging him. One night in the course of a bout in bed with a medical student from Tufts, he stopped, unwound the girl's legs, lumbered over to the phone and called Jessup at home. It was after midnight, and

Jessup had been asleep since ten. "Eddie," said Parrish, "let's do a half-life determination. We didn't destroy some of those rats for an hour. Who knows how long that stuff can sit in their brains? We should've done that long ago. I'd like to know its half-life. I'd like to know the transport system. I'd like to know how it passes the blood-brain barrier. I'd like to find some analogues."

"Okay, okay," yawned Jessup. "We won't have the use of the isolation tank for another three weeks anyway."

Jessup was, in point of fact, having his troubles arranging for the use of the isolation-tank room in the basement of B Building in the medical school complex. Not that the isolation tank was being used that much. In fact, it wasn't being used at all. Isolation tanks had gone out of fashion in the late 1960s, at least on the East Coast. The tank room had been locked for a long time, and nobody knew who held the key, not even the superintendent of the building. Jessup finally tracked it down to the Harvard Center of Cognitive Studies. When he got into the room, he found it had been used for odd storage. Considerable repairs had to be made. They had to rewire the tank for audio and polygraph recording, and the soundproofing of the room required some caulking. The tank itself was a little smaller than the ones Jessup had used in Maryland and at the Cornell Medical College, and consequently more coffinlike. It was an old-fashioned one with a hinged lid. The sides of the tank were only four feet high. Only a foot and a half of water was needed. It was not until Wednesday afternoon, the seventh of January, that Jessup was to go into the tank.

Meanwhile, they were shooting up dozens of rats with

the mixture, trying to determine how long it stayed in the system, how it moved through the body, whether it remained in the limbic system, and what similarities it had to any other chemicals or chemical compounds. It clearly had a synergistic effect. That is to say, none of the individual chemicals could account for the curious behavior of the compound. The individual chemicals, when injected into the rats, were not retrieved, had clearly been degraded in the body and came back as a by-product. However, they had yet to determine whether the synergism required the whole mixture or only a combination of two or three or four of the constituent chemicals. They hadn't even embarked on such a series of tests; it could take months. By now, Parrish was spending several hours a day on the compound, and he was grumpy about it. "I'm spending more time on this dumb compound," he grumbled, "than I am on my own dumb stuff."

On Tuesday, January 6, they got the printouts from x-ray crystallography. The results were not satisfying. The labeled substances did seem to bind to the DNA; on the other hand, no significant alteration was discovered. It was just after 6 P.M. that Parrish called Jessup at home to tell him about it.

"There was no alteration in the DNA?" Jessup asked.

"No. But I don't think you ought to take any more of that stuff. This ain't LSD, goddammit. This ain't no serotonin antagonist. How many grams of that stuff do you figure you've already got in you—two, three? You could be working up one hell of a case of cancer with a truckful of antimetabolites in you like that! This shit has fantastic stay-ing powers."

"Oh, come on, Mason, we've got half a dozen rats with a whopping load of that shit in them, and none of them have been adversely affected."

"Look, I don't think you ought to take any more of that shit until we finish breaking it down. When are you going to have that isolation-tank room ready?"

"Tomorrow."

"Tomorrow!"

"Didn't Arthur tell you?"

Parrish turned to Rosenberg who was sitting at the far end of his office. "What the hell is this about tomorrow?"

"I told you yesterday he had the tank room all fixed up."

"Well, you're not going to let him take any more of that damned compound, are you?"

Rosenberg puffed his pipe and took a long moment for contemplation. He folded his hands in his lap just below his burgeoning little paunch and smiled a brief smile. "We've got a sweet little problem here, Mason," he murmured, "with some fascinating speculations. Large amounts of the stuff localized in the hippocampus. Significant traces in the hypothalamic and pituitary axis and in the region of the pineal gland, but densely concentrated in the hippocampus. The EEG readings go straight to theta. No spindling, noth-ing. The hippocampus is particularly related to theta waves. There is some evidence that if you modify the theta rhythm, you may be able to modify the perception of time. So this substance may have some kind of time link. The limbic system just might be the seat of our deepest prenatal recall. Certainly, this substance induces hallucinations that have to be considered primordial." He looked up at Parrish, his eyes bright with curiosity, the slight, pensive smile trembling on his lips. "Yes, I'd like to pursue this inquiry another step. I'd like to see what happens if Eddie took another two hundred milligrams and went into the tank and programmed himself into early time. What the hell, another two hundred milligrams isn't going to kill him. Aren't you even a little curious?"

Parrish regarded Rosenberg coldly. "Well, you guys go ahead. You're behaving irresponsibly, and you're both going to get your ass in a sling. But not me." He returned his attention to the telephone. "I'm sorry, Eddie," he told Jessup. "I've got the computer room booked for tomorrow afternoon, and I've got two weeks' work backed up on me on account of your goddamned drug. So I'm not going to join you in your goddamned tank room. In fact, I don't want to see either of you guys for a long time." He slammed the receiver back into its cradle, turned to Rosenberg. "If it gets out you guys are testing on human subjects without an IND, you're going to get your ass in a sling, you know that, don't you? You guys are behaving in a fucking very unscientific manner, in violation of every canon of responsible research, and I don't want any part of your dumb experiments. So don't expect me tomorrow afternoon, and don't expect me from now on. In fact, I'd like to drop out of this whole mess."

That night, at two o'clock in the morning, according to Jessup's notes for January 7, 1976, he had a psychedelic flashback. He awoke in a bolt of terror, under the impression that small animals were crawling all over him, feeding on him. He threw off his blanket and saw his body swelling and contorting as if forces inside his body were about to break through the surface. An arm, for example, briefly shriveled into a bent little furred limb, much like a rat's paw. Suddenly, his feet were webbed, and then as suddenly transformed into furless protohuman feet. His skull ached, and when he touched it, he felt the bones of his skull, especially his jaw and those just above his eyebrows, reassembling into new formations beneath his skin. He experienced several shocks at the base of his skull. His chest surged into massive musculature and a second later shrank into that of some curious little arboreal animal. All this while, he was lying rigidly on his back, wearing only pajama trousers, completely awake. There was no question about that. The images were eidetic and undreamlike.

He had a girl with him that night, one of Parrish's seraglio of second-year medical students. She was roused by the initial commotion of his waking up, and sleepily asked him if he was all right. He answered yes. By a great effort of will, he got off the bed and promptly fell to his knees, not out of fear or weakness but because of a spinal compulsion to assume a more pronograde posture.

A moment later, he was able to stand again and he made his way carefully to the bathroom, where he closed the door, turned on the light and examined himself in the full-length mirror. All the while, his body continued to rumble, crack and buckle, and what he saw reflected in the glaring yellow light of the bathroom mirror was a series of disjunctive evolutionary images of himself, flickering one after another in the mirror, none of the images lasting more than a second. The images were mostly hominid and protohuman, what he took to be Ramapithecine figures, but several of the reflections showed him in the shape of a delicately fingered, insect-eating, lemur-like animal, perched in a tree, clutching a branch, and staring out through enormous soft eyes.

The whole experience couldn't have lasted more than thirty seconds, and suddenly it was over. He stood in the bathroom staring at his slight, white body, immobilized but oddly exhilarated. His girl had apparently gotten out of bed. She called to him through the closed bathroom door. "Are you all right, Eddie?" "I'm fine, I'm fine," he reassured her. To forestall further inquiry, he came out of the bathroom and headed for the living room. "I just want to make a few notes," he said, turning on the living room light. He sat at his desk and began to write down notes on the experience in his neat, cramped handwriting. For a moment, he had to pause, because his naked right arm lying on the desk abruptly released a protoplasmic substance, which moved up under the skin like a mole and disappeared into his elbow. He regarded this phenomenon in blank astonishment and then returned to his notes. After he finished, he went back to bed and fell into a profound sleep.

At a quarter after four that Wednesday afternoon, Mason Parrish decided to go to the tank room after all. He had to admit he was interested, how could he not be? Something within him told him not to go, some deep sense of impending trouble, even horror, a sort of penetrating intuitive feeling he was not usually given to. But he went anyway. He left the computer room with only half his work done, put his sheepskin jacket on over his long white lab coat, and went lumbering across the medical school quadrangle, hunched against the chill January air and the gathering dark gray of coming nightfall. He climbed the steps into B Building, went down a flight to the basement, and after asking two scurrying undergraduates where the isolation-tank room was, finally found it halfway down the length of a locker-lined, crate-and-box-filled corridor. He opened the door and went in. There was a good-sized monitoring room, space for four or five people who might wish to observe. Jessup and Rosenberg had installed some of their own portable equipment, an EEG machine, an intercom with earphones. His friends' coats were piled in a corner. Parrish unbuttoned his own and added it to the pile. A large one-way window looked into the tank room itself, which was quite dark, with just enough light for him to make out the tank which dominated the room, standing as it did squarely in the middle, eight feet long and painted black. Parrish had never seen an isolation tank before, and it looked to him very much like a plain coffin. Jessup must have climbed in already. Rosenberg was on a little footstool, bent over the tank, and was affixing EEG leads to Jessup's skull. Parrish opened the door that separated the two rooms and went into the tank room. Rosenberg looked up. "Look who's here" he smiled. "Couldn't resist, right?"

"Just had to see what kind of sorcery you guys were up to," said Parrish.

He looked over the edge of the tank. Jessup lay there, floating nakedly just below the surface of the inky water, motionless, a faint, almost imperceptible, shimmering white blob, like a huge dead fish with its belly up. His ankles were resting on what seemed to be a surgical dam, apparently built in to keep his feet from sinking. His stark white face, made even more grotesque by the EEG leads poking out of him, smiled up at Parrish, and he waggled a few fingers in welcome.

"Glad you came, Mason," he murmured.

"What've you got in there, some kind of salt solution?" asked Parrish.

"Ten percent magnesium sulfate," said Rosenberg, finished now with his EEG preparations. He carefully fed out the lead lines through tiny furrows along the wall of the tank and climbed down off the footstool. "Help me with the lid, Mason."

The aluminum lid of the tank was leaning in the black shadows against a wall. Rosenberg brought it over and between the two of them they carefully fitted it atop the tank. The head section of the lid, Parrish noted, was hinged. Parrish had a sudden moment of identification with Jessup, saw himself lying in the tank as the lid came down and a shocking blackness descended on and engulfed him.

"Weird, man," he commented in a low voice to Rosenberg, who was now leading him back to the control room.

Rosenberg clicked the intercom on, muttered into the mike: "One-two-three-four."

"One-two-three-four," answered Jessup's voice over the speaker.

"Okay, you're fine," said Rosenberg. He clicked the tape recorder on, murmured into it: "Wednesday, January seventh, nineteen seventy-six, four twenty-eight P.M." He pulled out a paperback mystery novel from his denim hip pocket, perched on the stool and began to read.

Parrish stood at the window, looking into the dark tank room, his hands thrust into the pockets of his lab coat, troubled by the austerity of that black coffin barely visible in the penumbral shadows of the room.

"Did he take the stuff already?" he asked Rosenberg.

"Oh, sure, about fifteen minutes ago."

Inside the tank, Jessup, white and naked, lay motionless, letting his body subside into its own tranquillity, watching the blackness turn even blacker, feeling his breathing get shallower and more resonant until the breathing was a form in itself, an endless amplification of itself, until all of space seemed to be made of it; then, suddenly, utter-shocking silence. A flick of an image penetrated the spaceless blackness: a promontory of columnar basalt. Another image: a black sea slowly subsiding, sinking, draining down. Black silence again. Another glimpsed image: a plain, undulating barrenly, covered with crushed rock. Again the subsiding sea and the sensation of sinking into it. Dense, black silence again.

In the monitoring room, Rosenberg read and Parrish sat hunched forward on a folding wooden chair, the tools of his trade poking out of his pockets—a stethoscope, an ophthalmoscope, fountain pens, a penlight. At 4:47 P.M., Jessup's voice issuing from the speaker aroused them both. "Okay," it intoned.

Rosenberg murmured into the tape recorder: "Centeredness at four forty-seven P.M." He noted the cassette was running low and prepared a second tape deck.

"What happens now?" whispered Parrish.

Rosenberg was about to answer when Jessup's voice chanted over the speaker: "Lots of disjunct but very precise images—beetles, maggots, dung flies, swooping birds with toothed beaks, grebes, geese, vultures, shearwaters, boobies, gannets—a flightless bird, somewhat like an ostrich, but easily more than ten feet tall, a marsupial mole, a beaver the size of a bear—clearly, I'm in some kind of primeval timespace—I'm picking up terrain now, it's terrific—broad-leaved tropical evergreens, palm trees, banana trees, jujube trees, sedge and spear grass—oh, it's terrific! a plateau or a lowland, grasslands, savannas—it's total now, completely focused, utterly real, no hallucination, I feel I'm actually alive and inside this landscape—a density of woodlands about a mile away, beyond that mountains that seem to be smoking, newly born mountains, Cenozoic, latter Tertiary, I'm in an edge area—utter tranquillity, but alive, life in the trees, life in the sedge, paradise, the garden of Eden, oh, my God! the birth of man! That's it! The birth of man! That's got to be it! It's a certainty! My God! There it is! A protohuman! The first and original truly human form! Tiny! Perhaps four feet high! Barely visible above the sedge grass! Completely furred, chimp-like, but erect, no knuckle-walking, shorter arms, moving along rather gracefully—there's two, three of them! Short legs, but bipedal, unformed feet, still simian, unformed arch, still moving along through the high grass, tiny, little furred humanoid creatures, a rock, some kind of basaltic rock, a chunk of lava in their hands, they're stalking or hunting, that's it! it's a hunt, they're hunting something— it's me! It's me they're hunting! It's me! Beautiful! Beautiful! I'm racing through the grass! I'm trying to get to the trees! They're on my flank! I'm struck by a stone! I'm down! They're on me! No, just one of them! It's his kill! The others have to wait their portion! He's beating me with his jagged chunk of lava! He's gouging gobbets of me with his chunk of lava, gibbing my guts! No pain! No pain! I tell you, no pain! He's devouring me! Ripping at my flesh! Clawing away my integumentation! Of course! It's me! It's my primordial me devouring me! I'm returning to my original me! Unbelievable sensation! Ineffable! Beatitude! Absolutely transcendental! I'm it, and it's me! I'm hunting! I'm killing! I'm eating! I'm eating the blood-hot flesh of a giant goat! Pure, ultimate hunger! Unbridled, natural, creature hunger! The id! The incarnated id!" At which, the near-hysterical fluency of Jessup's report on the intercom broke into a curious croak and then a series of quick clicking noises and then a strange, strangulated sort of howl.

It was too much for Parrish. He wrenched the door to the tank room open, crossed quickly to the tank and pulled the head section up.

Staring up at him from the blackness of the tank was Jessup's white face, as serene as a saint's. "Are you okay?" he asked the white face.

"Terrific, terrific," murmured the white face.

By now, Rosenberg was right behind Parrish, leaning over the tank. "Do you want to come down?" he asked Jessup's face.

"No."

Rosenberg slowly lowered the hinged lid, shrugged and headed back for the monitor room. After a moment, Parrish followed, closing the door slowly after himself. "Sounded like he was having a bad trip to me," he said to Rosenberg.

"Some of these tank trips can get pretty creepy," conceded Rosenberg.

He perched on the stool again, replaced his headset on his ears. Parrish sank down onto the wooden chair, feeling very jumpy.

Suddenly, the speaker emitted another of the croaking grunts, a series of clicking sounds and then some lip-smacking sounds. Parrish rose nervously to his feet. Rosenberg murmured into the mike: "You okay?"

"Beautiful," returned Jessup's soft voice.

Jessup didn't record another sound for the rest of the session (which went on for three and a half more hours) except in direct response to Rosenberg's anxious inquiries. The tapes rolled silently on. When you listen to the tapes, you hear nothing but the audio hum for periods of time as long as forty minutes and then you will hear Rosenberg's voice murmuring, "Can you hear me, Eddie?" "Yes." "Are you all right?" Rosenberg murmurs. "Yes." "What's going on? Fill me in," comes Rosenberg's murmur. Silence. "Are you sure you're okay?" asks Rosenberg. "Yes." "Do you want to stop this?" "No." "Do you want me to just leave you alone?" "Yes."

Jessup didn't come down from the trip until 8:46, when his voice suddenly made a strange grunt in Rosenberg's earphones. Rosenberg put his mystery novel down and murmured into the mike: "Are you okay, Eddie?" On the tape you now hear a soft creaking, which has to be interpreted as Jessup raising the hinge of his lid. Because when Rosenberg and Parrish went into the tank room, Jessup was just climbing out of the tank, into the subdued darkness of the tank room. Parrish handed him his hooded terry-cloth robe, and Jessup began toweling his hair.

Rosenberg said, "I don't like being out of contact for these long periods of time, Eddie."

Jessup nodded, toweled himself, a strange, monkish figure in the shadowed room, shrouded in the dark robe, its hood cowled over his head, only his white, wet eyes visible in the coped blackness of his face. The others were suddenly aware he was trying to say something. His jaws moved, but nothing came out except a rasping kind of grunt. His eyes stared mutely at them. He tried to talk again, but could produce only some clicking sounds. He sank slowly to his knees, his faceless white wet eyes staring in blank shock out of the black oval formed by the robe's cowl.

Parrish reached over and pulled the hood of the robe back. It seemed in the near-darkness of the room that Jessup's face was bearded with blood. Rosenberg turned the lights in the tank room on, and in the abrupt yellow light, there was Jessup on his knees in the middle of the room, his robe hanging limply on his white body, his face staring up, his cheeks and mouth wet with red blood, smeared where he had toweled his face, looking for all the world as if he had recently ravened a carcass.

"Christ, he must've bit his lip," said Parrish, and began

toweling away the blood. He felt Rosenberg's tentative hand on his shoulder, looked up.

"Do you want to take a sample of that blood?" said Rosenberg.

"Why?" said Parrish. The two men stared at each other. "Oh, for God's sake," snapped Parrish, "don't be weird." He slipped out of his lab coat, stripped off his T-shirt, wet it in the tank and used it to clean Jessup's face; some of the blood had caked. There were no lacerations on the lips, and when he poked his examining light into Jessup's mouth and up his nose, he couldn't find any active site of bleeding anywhere. "Must've had a seizure, hit his head or something," he muttered, more to himself than to anyone else. Throughout all this, Jessup was on his knees, clearly in a state of shock, staring mutely up into unseen spaces, his mouth agape. "Jesus Christ," muttered Parrish, who had been squatting on his haunches to do the examination. He rose with a creaking of limbs and began palpating Jessup's head, looking for gashes or anything else to explain the blood. Apparently, Jessup was coming out of the shock. He seemed to be trying to talk again, unsuccessfully. His jaws and mouth worked, but all that came out was a whistle and a clicking sound. He reached out his hand to Rosenberg to be helped up. Between his two friends, they finally got him standing. He seemed all right. The shock was clearly gone. The eyes responded intelligently, indeed they glinted with excitement. He seemed even to be smiling ever so briefly. He indicated that he couldn't talk and made motions to show that he wanted to write, and then briskly led the others back into the monitor room where he sat down on the wooden folding chair and began to scrawl on Rosenberg's notebook. Rosenberg leaned forward to read the message aloud. "'I can't talk except for these vocalizations.'"

"Can you hear me? Can you understand me?" asked Parrish.

Jessup nodded impatiently, scrawled another message. Rosenberg looked at the notebook. "What do you want blood tests for?" he asked.

Jessup was clearly frustrated and annoyed by this clumsy form of communication. When Parrish leaned to him to palpate his neck, he brushed his hand away angrily. He scrawled furiously in the notebook again.

"What's he say?" asked Parrish.

"He says," said Rosenberg, reading from the notebook, "'I want a buccal smear taken and blood for a karyotype. I want blood samples taken and sent to the Goodman and Sarich labs. I want some pictures of my neck. I want a whole series of films! Now! Before I reconstitute! Exclamation point.'"

"Before he what?" asked Parrish, slipping back into his long doctor's coat.

"Before he reconstitutes."

"Well, take his fucking blood," said Parrish, "and maybe he'll let me take a look at him."

Jessup, obviously in an agitated state, rolled the short sleeve of his robe up and stuck out his left arm to Rosenberg. His expression was imperious. Rosenberg fetched a Vacutainer and some tubes and a rubber tourniquet from an airline bag and set about taking blood samples, five tubes' worth.

"Do you mind," said Parrish to Jessup, "if I examine your neck for a minute?"

Jessup rolled his eyes in exasperation but allowed Parrish to palpate his neck.

"Any masses?" asked Rosenberg.

"No," grumbled Parrish. He fetched his stethoscope out of his coat pocket and auscultated Jessup's neck. From his scowl, his findings were patently puzzling—no bruits, no sounds of obstruction. He shone his ophthalmoscope into Jessup's eyes; apparently no papilledema either. Jessup submitted to all this with very little grace and only because he was confined by Rosenberg's drawing blood from his left arm. He sat on the wooden chair in his bulky robe, his legs crossed, one swinging nervously. His face was flushed with the effort of containing his inner turmoil. When Parrish asked him to do some perfunctory tests, such as stretching his right hand out, he pushed Parrish away and began scrawling a long passage in Rosenberg's notebook with his right hand. It read: *For God's sake, Mason, this is obviously no instance of common aphasia! Those noises I've been making are the same damned noises I made during the hallucinatory experience! It must be some kind of time-space fallout from the hallucination!*

"Oh, stop talking shit!" bellowed Parrish. "Are you saying your dumb hallucination has externalized?"

"What'd he write?" asked Rosenberg, inserting the last tube into the Vacutainer.

Parrish read Jessup's last message aloud. After which he leaned down to stare nose to nose at Jessup and said, "You are a fucking flake, Jessup, so get dressed and I'm taking you over to the Brigham and do a complete workup on you!"

Jessup shook his head.

"You are a very sick dude, you dumb son of a bitch!" shouted Parrish. "And I want to look down your throat, get some skull films, do a CAT scan, maybe even an arteriogram, and I'd like an unbiased eye to look at those EEG tracings!"

Jessup sat primly on his chair, the robe tucked demurely over his knees, apparently calm now but unrelenting. He shook his head a very clear no. Rosenberg had finished drawing blood by now and was labeling the tubes. Jessup was sitting with his left arm doubled up to clot the flow of blood. With his right arm, he wrote in Rosenberg's notebook: *Just x-rays.*

"Okay," muttered Parrish. "Get your clothes on, and let's get over to x-ray."

"They lock the hospital doors at five-thirty," said Rosenberg. "We'll have to go through the tunnels."

The three of them went trudging through the sub-basement tunnels, long, deserted, sinuous catacombs, Dantean at that hour of the night. These were the bowels of the buildings, where the maintenance and incinerator rooms were. The walls were lined with huge, thick, hot-water pipes, and as they passed the open incinerators, flames leaped up from the depths of the incinerator wells, dug a hundred feet into the foundations of the building. They made a quixotic trio, shambling, bulky Parrish in his long white doctor's coat, tiny Rosenberg in a torn sweater, carrying his little blue airline bag, and Jessup in Levi's, his shirt-tails not entirely tucked in.

Rosenberg muttered to Parrish, "Maybe he's an akinetic mutant."

"Don't be a schmuck," snorted Parrish. "He's moving, isn't he? He's responsive."

"Is it possible it's purely mechanical?"

"Well, neurologically, he's grossly intact," Parrish said, scowling, "and, if it isn't neurological, then it's got to be mechanical. I'd like to at least get a look at his cords, the stupid nut, and do a barium swallow. Maybe I'll run down to Emergency and pick up an ENT bag."

When they got to the hospital buildings, they climbed a flight of stairs to the Brigham's radiology department. Parrish had to pull a little rank to get the x-rays done. "Take some plain films of his neck," he told the technician. "I want a PA, a lateral and an oblique."

"Jesus, Doctor," whined the technician, "I'm backed up to my ass for tonight—"

"Take the damn pictures!" snapped Parrish. "This is an emergency!"

The technician took Jessup into the x-ray room. Parrish leaned back against the wall of the outside room and scowled. "Listen, Arthur," he said in a low voice, "don't tell Eddie he had blood on his face when he came out of the tank. He'll give us all kinds of shit that he got the blood from eating that goat in his hallucination. He'll want to take blood samples off my shirt and that robe of his. And I don't think I can take any more of his dumb witchcraft shit. So don't tell him about it because I think he's about ready to crack up altogether, and we're going to wind up dragging him to Mass Mental."

"What do you think it is?"

Parrish fished out a cigar from his breast pocket, unwrapped it, lit it. "He's not the type for a hysterical conversion, so I'm thinking seizure. He came out of the tank in a fugue state, and he had blood all over his face. He must've had a seizure in the tank, bit his tongue while convulsing, and is post-icticly aphasic. I thought maybe he had a vascular insult, a TIA stroke or flipped an embolus. But neurologically he's intact, so I'm thinking seizure now. Did you bring those EEG tracings with you?"

"No, I left them in the tank room."

"We'll pick them up on the way back when we get the coats."

"We'll have to clean up back there, you know. You left your shirt with all that blood on it and Eddie's robe."

"Yeah, I know."

The x-rays the technician brought out gave them quite a turn, all except Jessup, who mutely but with manifest delight pointed out that the hyoid bone seemed to be elevated, the base of the tongue broadened and the pharyngeal space shorter than is normally found.

"Take it easy," growled Parrish. "None of us are that terrific at reading x-rays."

"What're you guys looking for?" asked the technician.

"Look," said Parrish, "I'd like to see what he looks like under fluoro. You got any barium around here?"

They all went into the x-ray room and fluoroscoped Jessup. There were no obstructions or masses.

It was half-past eleven when they left the radiology department and headed back for the tank room. They trudged along silently through the deserted subbasement tunnels, each deep in his own thoughts. They went into the tank room to gather their coats. Rosenberg reassembled the portable EEG machine and trundled it into the outer corridor. Parrish gathered up the blood-smeared terry-cloth robe and his blood-caked T-shirt, rolled them into a large ball and stuck it under his arm. When he came back into the monitor room, Jessup was seated quietly on the wooden chair, his sheepskin coat already on. Parrish pointed to the robe under his arm. "Do you want me to get this cleaned for you?"

"Yes," said Jessup. "I'd appreciate that, Mason."

It took Parrish a full five seconds to realize Jessup had regained his voice. He relit his cigar, looked out into the corridor to see where Rosenberg had got to. Then he wheeled around back into the monitor room and gaped at Jessup. "Are you okay?" he asked.

"I'm fine, Mason," said Jessup. "I knew this was just a transient thing."

"A transient ischemic attack, that's what it was," said Parrish. Rosenberg came back into the room. "He's got his voice back," said Parrish.

"It wasn't an ischemic attack; it has nothing to do with blood flow; there was no mass," said Jessup. "And it wasn't a seizure. I'm telling you what it was. I programmed myself into latter Tertiary space and physically entered my own hallucination, and I came out of that tank with the hallucination spilling over into external reality for a couple of hours. There was an overlap in time perception, and I briefly retained physical vestiges of the hallucination. I don't know, we may be into some kind of quantum thing here, or some exotic relativistic physics, in which consciousness snapped me into some new sharp state. My physics is lousy. Do you guys know any of those quantum flakes out at MIT we could pose this problem to?"

The others just stared at him.

"For God's sake," continued Jessup, "those strange vocalizations I was making were the first formations of human speech. I obviously reverted to some protohuman state. You saw the x-rays, Mason. There was a clear fusion of the digastric muscles to the hyoid bone, and the larynx was in an unusually forward position. I'm not sure, but I think the digastric muscles, which are looped in humans, are fused directly to the hyoid bones in apes. If so, then I obviously regressed to some quasi-simian creature."

It had been a bad night for Parrish, and he was beginning to lose his temper. He glanced over to Rosenberg, who was packing up the tape recorders and the polygraph machines. "Arthur," he said tightly, "give me those x-rays. I'd like to show them to somebody who can read them right. We're reading them wrong, that's all there is to it. Because nobody's going to tell me you de-differentiated your goddam genetic structure for four goddam hours and then reconstituted!" He took the folder of x-rays from Rosenberg's hand. "I'm a professor of endocrinology at the Harvard Medical School. I'm an attending physician at the Peter Bent Brigham Hospital, a consulting editor to the *American Journal of Endocrinology*, a fellow and vice-president of the Eastern Association of Endocrinologists . . ." He erupted into full-blown rage, his face beet red with the effort. ". . . and I'm not going to listen to any more of your cabalistic, quantum, frigging, limbo-state, dumb mumbo-jumbo! I'm going to show these goddam dumb x-rays to a radiologist! And I'm going to show them to him right now, as soon as I can get my ass over to whoever is reading tonight at the radiology department! Give me my fucking coat, Arthur! I hope I never see either of you two bastards again!"

He seized his coat from Rosenberg's outstretched hand, wrenched the corridor door open and strode out, holding the bundle of bloodied clothing under one arm and his sheepskin coat under the other and clutching the brown envelope containing the x-rays. He went striding massively down the deserted, litter-filled subbasement tunnels to the Brigham's basement, mounted a flight of stairs, swept through the swinging doors of the East Hall, and marched into the Department of Radiology, where an unhappy resident was poring over a stack of x-ray pictures. Parrish took a deep breath, extended the envelope to the radiologist and managed to say in a reasonably calm voice, "Do me a favor, take a look at these."

The radiologist scowled at this odd interruption, then extracted the films from the envelope. "What's the story in this case?" he asked.

"Thirty-five-year-old white man, acute onset of aphasia, no history of trauma."

The radiologist affixed the x-rays against the light. "What're you looking for?" he asked.

"It looks to me like the architecture is somewhat abnormal."

"Somewhat?" said the radiologist, peering at the films. "This guy's a fucking gorilla."

Parrish went wandering aimlessly through the dark subbasement tunnels of the hospital. He had put on his coat, but was still carrying the bundled-up terry-cloth robe under one arm and the envelope of x-rays in the hand of the other. For a moment, he paused outside a black incinerator room. There were two incinerator wells, one of which was flaring with flames. The rest of the room was empty but for battered cans of rubbish and a variety of empty crates and cartons and other litter waiting to be disposed of. He looked back up the corridor; it was deserted. He walked to the smoking incinerator well. A quick flutter of orange flame leaped out at him. He crushed the bloody robe and shirt into a ball and, with a pretense of unconcern, threw it down into the flames.

Outside, a soft January snow had begun to fall. It fell softly on the medical school complex, the ancient towers of the Brigham Hospital, the endless construction work being done on old Vanderbilt Hall, on the occasional car with its swishing windshield wipers. Parrish trudged across the dark, deserted white streets to the trolley stop on Huntington Avenue, numbed by shame.

Cambridge, Harvard
Medical School,
Van Buren
Park Zoo
April 1976

Emily and the girls returned from Africa on Good Friday, April 16, a crisp, bright, sunny day. Jessup met them at the airport, anxious, even resentful. He had had to cancel his two o'clock class, an elective called The Methodology of Consciousness, and little changes in routine made him feel dislodged, derailed. On the other hand, your wife and kids come back after a year's absence, separated or not, it was merely civil that you meet them, help with the luggage, get them into their new home. The plain fact was that he had sorely missed them. He was an isolated man, but it was precisely because of his solitariness that he had missed them. Even solitariness demands a structure, someone in the next room one can retreat from. He had been too alone, often bored with himself. During his seven years of marriage, he had lived with a relentlessly simmering rage directed against his wife's disorderliness: torn drapes and stuffing coming out of the arms of chairs, diapers and toys constantly underfoot; late afternoon calls at his office or lab, his wife saying: "Listen, I won't have time for dinner, can you bring home something from the deli?"; the demands of domestic minutiae, the childhood illnesses of his children, humbug chats with the pediatrician, the whole preposterous imprisonment of marriage and fatherhood. But once he was left alone and free and the house tidied up and everything clinically in its place, he had found that the rage still simmered, unfocused now, a formless seething rage he found very hard to contain at times, times in which he suspected himself of imminent madness, a sensation of horror just on the periphery of his civilized sanity, a horror moving about like a lurking pack of predatory animals in the darkness of the primeval forest. So the rage hadn't been caused by the torn curtains and the torn chairs and the delicatessen meals and the diapers and the boxes of Tampax in the bathroom. The rage was his alone, had always been his.

When Emily finally got through customs and came filing down the tunnel with the two girls, she spotted Jessup immediately on the other side of the gate, standing there like any other husband and father, a welcoming smile on his face, his eyes bright, perhaps too bright, with enthusiasm. He began shouldering his way through the crush of people at the gate and embraced her vigorously, and then embraced the kids, first individually and then in tandem, and then back to her again, holding her tightly. He had an erection the size of a house, and there were tears in his eyes. "Oh, brother," he kept muttering. "My God—you all look so wonderful!"

Indeed they did, browned by a year of African sun. Emily was wearing a cheeky little safari skirt because she knew she had sensational legs. Still, she was startled by the exuberance of Jessup's greeting, especially the tears. He scooped up three-year-old Margaret and began pushing the cart loaded with their baggage toward the exits, shouting at his older daughter as he went, "Come on, Grace! Let's get this luggage home! I know you have a present for me, and I want to see it!" He suddenly paused, whirled around, and stared at his six-year-old, who had been racing after him and had come to a squealing, giggling halt. He bent forward and looked her in the eye with mock sternness. "You did bring me a present, didn't you?"

"Yes!" squealed the delighted little girl.

"Very well then," said Jessup, and he turned on his heel and went striding off again.

All around the arrival area, people had turned to watch this jolly scene with doting smiles. It was exactly the sort of artificially happy little domestic moment, Emily thought, that Jessup would have detested a year ago. She followed along after them, beginning to wonder if, in fact, Jessup was on the verge of madness, as Mason Parrish had written her. The whole episode had been so remarkably atypical.

There was a great deal of luggage. Jessup lashed some on the roof of his Toyota, stuffed some into the trunk of the car and the rest on the seats so that Grace, riding in the back with her mother, sat on a suitcase, and Margaret, in front, was crushed up against her father's elbow. It was a twenty-minute ride to Cambridge across the glinting Charles River. The two girls stretched and twisted to look out the windows, scanning for familiar sights and complaining they recognized nothing. Emily, in the back, her long brown legs crossed, chattily reported on her year's work in Africa.

It had been a good year for Emily. She had spent nearly eleven months in careful observation of two troops of baboons on the Serengeti Plains, with particular interest in their call system. And she thought she had come back with some really terrific new information on how baboons communicate with each other. She had concluded among other things that baboons were not as generally a seed-gathering and insect-eating society as had been supposed and that their occasional ventures into carnivorousness were not as random as had been thought. She had personally witnessed six occasions of predation which had involved the primitive behavior of hunters. In two instances, a pair of baboons had killed young Thomson's gazelles and eaten them. There had been some kind of rudimentary communication between the two baboons that was noticeably different from the usual grunts, clicks and lip-smackings that marked other baboon exchanges. Emily could only surmise that if baboons had found meat-eating necessary for their survival as a species, they might well have gone on to an appreciation of tools as weapons of the hunt and developed other hominid patterns, even language. This was a pretty wild supposition and she wouldn't think of saying it publicly, but she thought she was on to something important. At any rate, she was especially interested right now in the recent work on nonverbal communication being done with chimpanzees. Chimpanzees are the closest of the great apes to man, and there was a good body of recent evidence that chimps were capable of symbolic communication, notably the work being done by Alan and Trixie Gardner at the University of Nevada. She had been in correspondence with the Gardners and was thinking of flying out to visit them in a couple of weeks. She had nothing else to do all summer except write up her report.

"I don't suppose you recorded any of those baboon sounds," asked Jessup as he helped lug the baggage up the porch stairs of Emily's new home.

"Yes, of course I did, why?" asked Emily.

"I'd sure like to hear those tapes," said Jessup.

"Of course," said Emily, and unlatched the door.

Her home—that is to say, the new flat she had rented just prior to leaving for Africa—was the ground floor of a shambling white Cape Cod house on Warren Street, just two blocks off the Common. The landlord welcomed them from his second-floor window: "I opened your windows to air it all out," he called down. "And I had the company put in a telephone."

"Thank you, Mr. Lindsay." Emily beamed up at him, then proceeded into the foyer of the house.

Jessup held the front door open for the kids to lug their private parcels in. Mr. Lindsay came down the stairs to tell them he had stocked up some staples for them, to be found in the refrigerator. There was a great deal of smiling and saying, "God, it's good to be back." Emily suggested to Jessup that they unload the car and then all go into town for hamburgers and some grocery shopping; she could do all the unpacking later. From a living room window, she watched her husband lugging a bulging canvas Val Pak in one hand and with the other dragging a carton filled with books up the pathway to the front porch. He didn't seem very changed, a little thinner perhaps. She went out to the front door to help him. He swung the carton of books up onto the porch with a thud and looked up at her, sweating, smiling. She felt a surge of fondness for him.

"How've you been, Eddie?" she asked.

He took a strange little moment to consider his answer, frowned, suddenly smiled again. "I don't know," he said. "Strange things have been happening."

She was about to say that she knew, but thought better of it.

Around four o'clock that afternoon, the two girls were out on the sidewalk, reconnoitering the block for other children. Jessup sat at the kitchen table with a cup of coffee, and Emily sorted out the soiled laundry from a large canvas suitcase lying open in the middle of the kitchen floor. It had not taken long for Emily to reduce the whole flat to the splendid disarray she seemed to fancy. Cartons, small crates, valises, carrying bags lay open in every room, half emptied; clothing was piled on beds, in heaps on the floor; books and notebooks, cans of film and stacks of tape cassettes and reels were massed in mounds on beds, chairs and tables. She moved about through all this with some private pattern of efficiency, flicking on lights as the first shadows of dusk darkened the rooms. Jessup watched her come and go, bend and stretch, her saucy little ass ticking away under the brief skirt, exchanged passing smiles with her whenever they chanced to look at each other. She suddenly sat down at the kitchen table across from Jessup, poured herself a cup of coffee and said:

"I got a letter from Mason about a week ago, just before we left Nairobi. He says you've abandoned your old research and you and Milton Mitgang are now doing in vivo studies with schizophrenics at Mass Mental."

Jessup sipped his coffee but said nothing.

"And without clearance," added Emily.

"What else did Mason write you?"

"He says you talked Mitgang into going along with you by lying to him about the protocol being approved by the Research Committee. But you didn't get approval from any Research Committee or from his unit chief, did you? Mason says you're using a very complex drug which you brought up from Mexico; it hasn't been thoroughly tested yet and is dangerous as hell."

"As a matter of fact, Mitgang is very pleased with the studies. We've only been at it five weeks, but we've found decreased urine levels of dopaminergic metabolites. We also found N-methoxy-bufatonin in the urine serums, which is a melatonin analogue and a substance specific to schizophrenia and would support the toxic metabolite theory. Mitgang has always been hot for the toxic metabolite theory."

"For God's sake, Eddie, you can't do in vivo studies on human beings without clearance. You're going to get into terrible trouble."

"In fact, Mitgang is so infatuated with this drug, he

wants to try and sell the thing to Smith, Kline & French. He's a stage-four clinical consultant for them."

"Is Evans still Mitgang's unit chief? He's going to want to know why he doesn't have your protocol on file. You'll be up before the Ethics Committee. You'll both have your grants discontinued. You can lose your faculty appointment. You'll be lucky to get a job anywhere."

Jessup suddenly smashed his hand down on the table. The coffee cups clattered. He stared at Emily with what seemed to be blind rage.

"What else did Mason write you?" he roared.

Emily regarded him levelly. "He says that over the past year you've taken about two grams of that drug yourself and that you had a very unusual instance of genetic regression about three months ago, which he thinks was an incipient neoplastic process, and that you've probably got leukemia or lymphoma. He's been trying to get you into the hospital for a complete workup, but you refuse to go. He's worried stiff that you're cracking up. He thinks you've been behaving very strangely, and he begged me to talk to you about this when I got back."

Jessup sat in sullen silence for a moment. "Mason," he muttered, "is pathologically incapable of keeping his big mouth shut about anything."

"He's worried about you."

"He's also a stupid, starched, hidebound idiot."

"Mason is a first-rate doctor."

"He's a first-rate fatuous bigmouth!" snapped Jessup. "It's not leukemia or any other kind of cancer! I let him do a liver-spleen scan on me and a CAT scan. I've been probed, scoped and palpated! Parrish has had a mirror down my throat or up my ass every half hour for nearly three months! And there is no evidence, no suggestion whatsoever, of cancer!" He was standing now, flushed with fury, his hands visibly trembling with the effort of controlling the mounting rage within him. "How dare he write to you about it!" he shouted. "What else did he write to you? What else did he tell you? He was supposed to keep his mouth shut, that's what he was supposed to do! He wants to tell everybody!"

He suddenly strode off into the living room. Emily remained in the kitchen, her legs crossed, sipping her coffee, frowning with concern. As suddenly, Jessup was back again, standing in the doorway, shouting: "Why the hell should I go into the hospital? Do you think I want the whole goddamned staff of the Brigham in on this! My God! We're not the only people investigating consciousness and alteration of matter! There's Lowenstein at U-Cal-Irvine, the guy who just left Szent-Gyorgyi's group, who's trying to alter matter through biogenics. There's that guy at Kings-Cambridge who's picked up on all Northrop's stuff, altering matter through varying charge potentials. If he ever got wind that we had effected genetic change through manipulation of consciousness, Jesus, that son of a bitch will be publishing tomorrow, before I can even get to my typewriter. For God's sake, Emily, I don't have the money or the facilities to compete with all those guys at Cal and Michigan and Stanford. If we're going to foot-race those guys with all those fat grants, we'll be years behind. Their Nobel Prizes will be antiques before we even get started. We don't know what we've got yet, for God's sake! You don't go telling every sci-

entist in Boston about it! They'll steal it, for God's sake!
They'll steal it! I'll kill the son of a bitch next time I see him!
What else did he write you? What else did he tell you about
that genetic regression I went through three months ago?"

She didn't answer because she knew anything she said
would only elicit another outburst. After a moment of
weighted silence, she got up and went to the doorway. Jessup was poking about among the stacks of tape cassettes
and reels, piled by the porch window, trying to read the la-
bels in the insufficient light. Outside the window, the dusk
was gathering quickly. For the moment, the living room was
lit only by the bulb of one standing lamp with an orange
shade, and Jessup was in heavy shadow. He was hunched
over, a near silhouette in a gray ski sweater and shapeless
chino slacks, peering at the label on a can of film. He looked
up at her, his eyes catching the yellow light from the lamp.

"Which of these," he asked, "has the baboon vocalizations on them? I'd like to hear them."

"Why?"

He smiled. "As a matter of fact, we could use some of
your expertise. Did Mason write you that during that inci-
dent of regression I went through, I had an aphasic experience for about four hours? Absolutely inexplicable. For four
hours, my speech mechanisms physically regressed to some
primitive state, perhaps even simian. At the end of the four
hours, I reconstituted completely. You used to be a comparative anatomist. How good are you at reading x-rays?"

"Pretty good."

"We've got a whole series of them. In fact, we ran the
series twice. The geniohyoid muscle is severely swollen. The

pharynx is like sealed off. The digastric muscles are fused to the hyoid bone, that's simian, isn't it? Mason checked out the pictures with a radiologist. He thought it was a gorilla. During the course of the aphasia, the only sounds I could get out were clicks and grunts. I've got a gut hunch they're very much like the baboon vocalizations you have on your tapes. That's why I want to hear them."

"Do you have your vocalizations on tape?"

"Yes."

"I'd like to hear them."

"Do you understand what I'm trying to tell you?"

"I understand very well. You're telling me that three months ago, you had a four-hour period in which you genetically regressed to an ape. Mason says that during that four-hour period you took blood tests, and that both the Sarich and Goodman labs report the cellular-immune systems tests revealed characteristics of VAB and CEP blood group systems."

"On the other hand, they also picked up XG^a antigens, which are specific to man."

"I'd like to see that data."

"I'd like you to see it. We also ran regular tests. The serums and the CBC's were normal. There was a slightly abnormal differential in the white count, some hypersegmented nuclei in the polys, some rouleau formation, and a general increase in mytotic activity. And we also took a buccal smear. The chromosomal count was forty-eight—"

"Are you serious? That's nonhuman."

"—and was twenty-six percent chromatin positive, and the structure of the karyotype was also nonhuman."

They stood staring at each other across the living room. Margaret straggled into the room in her jeans and wrapped herself around her father's knees. Jessup fondled her towhead absently.

"Look, Emily," he said, "I'm not mad. I know Mason thinks I am, and so, probably, does Arthur, and God knows I've received enough nut mail—even Dean Medich had me down to his office, saying what sort of rubbish are you putting out—"

"When did this happen? How the hell did Dean Medich get into this? For God's sake, you didn't tell the dean about it!"

"Well, I wrote it up."

"What do you mean, you wrote it up?"

"I wrote it up for *PNAS*. Goddam Parrish was running around telling everybody in the world about it, so I thought I'd better get it published before somebody beat me to it. I just wanted to get it on record. I'm sorry now I did it. Lord knows, it was premature. But Parrish has this molecular biologist buddy out at MIT, and he took him all the hard data, and the next thing I knew, they had another radiologist in on it and a couple of other flakes out there at MIT. It was getting out of hand, so I wrote it up and sent it to *PNAS*. I didn't make a big deal out of it, just the hard data and an analysis of the drug mixture. Frankly, I didn't think anybody would pay that much attention to it, it's so wild."

"Wild! You published a paper saying you had taken a mysterious potion that turned you into an ape! Good God, Eddie! You're supposed to be one of the brightest stars in the world of physiology! You've made yourself ridiculous!"

"Look, Emily, an incomprehensible instance of regression has occurred, literal, physical regression: muscles, bones, chromosomes and genes. We have a small body of evidence here that cannot be explained away as leukemia or lymphoma. Because how do you explain that four hours later I had completely reconstituted? Every blood test, every scan and every test Mason can devise has shown me completely normal, every muscle, bone, chromosome and gene back in its proper human place. For four hours I had shown the physical properties of a man-ape. The next day, I was absolutely normal. So we're not talking about regression at all. I'm not even sure we're talking about alteration of matter. There was a transformation of biological structures, that's clear. But beyond that, we don't know what we've got. There's no way this can be explained in terms of biological time. In some way, we're penetrating time barriers. This is quantum stuff. We're in blue sky. We've got ourselves a singularity, a physical event that is out of context of all known theory. Like a black hole."

He was becoming agitated again. "Look, in purely physiological terms, I'm perfectly willing to concede the drug is triggering the DNA alterations, maybe by the codons. The basic structure is the same in terms of the nucleotides. It's how the relative sequence is read that's altered. Something has triggered some very old genes to work. Maybe the structural genes became operator genes and the regulators became repressors. And with every manner of vice versas. I'll bet you the bases of my DNA strands were lighting up like a pinball machine!" His daughter was tugging for attention at his trouser leg. He scooped her up and clutched her to him.

"Everybody thinks your father's going nuts," he whispered into her hair. He began striding around the shadowed room, holding the child close to him, talking in bursts like a man out of breath. "Mason argues that DNA damage doesn't reveal itself in the host, only in the progeny, but if you recall the first blood tests, there was a hell of a lot of intracellular activity. That doesn't prove anything, of course, but it's consistent with genetic mutation. Arthur argues it transiently alters the templates. What templates? The protein templates. Okay, I'll buy that, but what triggered that?" He began to shout again. "I mean, for God's sake, the thing to do is for me to get back in that isolation tank and try it again! Let's see if it happens again, for God's sake! I mean, none of us really believes it happened! After three months, I'm beginning to wonder myself if it ever happened! But oh, no! They won't go back in the tank! No; they're spending all their time fractionating rats' brains! What the hell am I supposed to do while they're fractionating rats' brains! So I got Mitgang to get up a patient group from his clinic. I mean, let's do some in vivo studies on humans! Let's see if this damned drug by itself will induce regression in humans! Well, I've been injecting that drug into twelve schizophrenics for five weeks now, and there has been not one single instance of regression! I am convinced the regression was triggered by an act of consciousness! While I was in the tank, I entered another consciousness! I became another self! A more primitive self! And the drug, in some way, triggered the externalization of that other, more primitive self!"

His daughter began to whimper.

"Put her down, Eddie," said Emily. "You're frightening her."

Jessup gently restored his daughter to the floor. Emily picked up the frightened child. When she looked again at her husband, he was sitting on the soft chair under the lamp, his eyes closed, his face masklike.

"At least look at my data," he muttered.

"Of course, Eddie. Maybe tomorrow afternoon. Would tomorrow afternoon be all right?"

"Don't patronize me," he said.

"I'm not—"

He stood up, shouting, "It's just possible I'm not mad, you know! I'm asking you to make a small quantum jump with me! To accept one deviant concept—that our other states of consciousness are as real as our waking state and that that reality can be externalized!"

"You're screaming."

"I know! But I've been getting this patronizing shit from Arthur and Mason for three months now, and I'm sick of it. You're all so hung up on time and space! The possibility that a ten-million-year-old substance can take physical form seems to terrify you. You've got to stop thinking about time and space as if they were inviolable. They are not inviolable! They do not exist in themselves! They are postulates of the conscious mind! They are properties of bodies in motion, intellectual concepts, necessary only for the measurements of mechanistic physics. There is no time and space in mathematics. There is no time in atomic physics or in intergalactic space. In outer space, there is no difference between a split second and a billion years! Why the hell should there be any difference in our inner space? We've got millions and millions of years stored away in that computer bank we call our minds! We've got trillions of dormant genes in us, our whole evolutionary past. Perhaps I've tapped into that! For God's sake, all I'm saying is I want to get back in that tank and repeat the experiment! The most elementary laboratory behavior! Repeat the experiment! Confirm it! Verify it! I would like other responsible scientists with me when I do it! I'd like a little consensual validation on this! And my God, if it's true, do you know what we've got? We will have exploded frontiers across the whole panoply of science! We may have demonstrated a whole new force in nature. There are some physicists who have spent their lives trying to demonstrate that consciousness can affect physical systems. Well, I might just have done that! I don't know how! I don't know why! But my God, don't you agree it merits further investigation? I mean, we're talking about an achievement comparable to Newton, Darwin, Einstein!"

He sat again, crossed his legs, folded his hands in his lap. The orange light of the lamp slashed across his face. He seemed composed and completely mad.

"Needless to say, Emily, don't talk to anyone about any of this," he said. "Scientists are a very curious breed. There isn't much money in science and very little celebrity. There is, however, a great deal of vainglory and a murderous thirst for immortality. There are scientists who will perjure, suborn, cheat, steal, swindle and even kill to get their names in the textbooks or to be standing up there in Stockholm in their cutaways, modestly accepting the Nobel Prize. So I would appreciate your saying nothing about this to anyone. I've got all the tapes, notes and everything at my place. What time would you like to come over and look at the stuff tomorrow?"

"Two, two-thirty?" She smiled nervously. "I just want to get Grace," she said. "I'll be right back."

She went out into the dark entrance foyer of the house, carrying Margaret, and let herself out onto the porch. It was near night now, but she could see Grace in front of a neighbor's house, talking to a woman with a very small boy. She started to call, but thought better of it and walked down the path to the sidewalk. She set Margaret on her feet, and they went to join the little group in front of the neighbor's house.

The woman smiled at her. "I'm Linda Sandys. I belong to that house over there." She pointed to a gray clapboard house across the darkening street and down the block.

"I'm Emily Jessup," said Emily.

"And you've just come back from Africa," said the woman. "I've been talking to Grace, who's been telling me and Georgie all about it. My husband's in French classics."

"I'm in anthropology," said Emily, her body as tense and bursting as if she were swaddled in corsets.

"So Grace has been telling me," smiled Mrs. Sandys. "Would you like to come over and have some coffee?"

"I'd love to, really," said Emily, "but I've got a hungry husband back in the house." She enfolded her two children. "We're going to a Chinese restaurant," she lied. Margaret promptly broke away and scampered down the sidewalk to her own house, as promptly followed by Grace. Emily took a step nervously after them. "We're still unpacking," she said.

"Of course." Mrs. Sandys smiled again.

"I'll take you up on that coffee tomorrow morning, if I may," said Emily.

"Please. The gray house there."

"Thank you, excuse me," said Emily and hurried back down the walk after her children.

When she got back to the house, both children were on the porch. Her heart leaped with fear. "Is your father all right?" she asked.

"Where is he?" asked Grace.

Emily went into the foyer, now almost black. She clicked on the hall light. The living room door was open, and she could see that the chair was empty. She knew instantly he was gone, but she entered the room, calling out, "Eddie?" She started to look in the kitchen, but instead went to the phone, hidden under a pile of children's clothing on the low bookcase, and dialed Mason Parrish's number. There was no answer. The two girls straggled in.

"Where is he?" asked Grace.

"I don't know," said Emily. "I guess he had an appointment." She dialed Arthur Rosenberg's number. Sylvia Rosenberg answered. "Sylvia, this is Emily Jessup. Is Arthur in? . . . When do you expect him? . . . Oh, I'm just fine, we're all just fine, we're still unpacking, and I've got to hang up. I'll call you later and tell you all about it. Please tell Arthur to call me as soon as he gets home. . . . Listen, you wouldn't happen to know where Mason is right now, would you? I just tried him at home, and he wasn't in. . . ." She stood there chatting away, numbed and frightened.

Around six o'clock that evening, Edward Jessup parked his Toyota in the Brigham parking lot. It had begun to drizzle. Jessup hunched his shoulders and, carrying Rosenberg's airline bag, crossed Shattuck Avenue to the medical school complex. He went into the administration building and down a flight of steps to the basement level, along the connecting corridor to B Building. The drizzle outside had filled the basement corridors with white-coated doctors and lounging clusters of medical students. He unlocked the isolation-tank room and went in, flicked on the lights in the monitor room and then opened the connecting door to the tank room, flicking on the lights there as well.

The large glass window to the monitor room was black and opaque. The room was bare except for a white porcelain bowl in the corner and, of course, the black-painted tank in the middle of the room. He turned on the water valve, and water began rumbling into the tank. He adjusted the thermostat, opened the airline bag, extracted a jar of magnesium sulfate and poured it into the gathering spume at the bottom of the tank. He stripped off his clothes, walked back to check the water level in the tank. He took a Mason jar of liquid out of the airline bag and measured off 4cc of the liquid into a syringe, then squirted that into a beaker. He drained the beaker in one gulp, walked over to pick up the porcelain basin, checking the water level again en route. He stood holding the basin, watching the tank fill up to the indentation that marked a foot and a half, and then he turned the valve off. He leaned against the tank, waiting. After a moment, he began to vomit into the basin. He walked around the room, naked except for his wrist watch, retching as the spasms overtook him. When that was done, he carefully set the white basin back into its corner, picked up the black lid of the tank and placed it against the tank. He checked his watch, returned to the airline bag, took out a legal pad of paper and wrote: *Went into the tank 6:22 P.M. April 16*. He stripped off his watch, dropped it on the pile of his clothing, picked up the lid, climbed into the tank and slowly sat down in the water, lowering the lid onto its hinges as he did. He left only the hinged headpiece open. With the lid in place, he lay back slowly in the inky water, motionless, letting his body subside, his eyes open, glistening white in the black rectangle of the opening at the head of the lid, as he listened to the silence grow silent. After a moment, he reached one white arm up and closed the headpiece of the lid, engulfing himself in utter blackness. He rested motionless again, feeling his breathing get shallower until the breathing was a form in itself and all of him and all his selves drifted together into the center of the breathing which had become the center of everything.

Sometime before half-past nine, he raised the hinged lid and climbed out of the tank with some effort, because when he clambered over the side into the subdued brownish-yellow light of the tank room, he was a finely furred creature barely four feet tall, bipedal if perhaps a bit sloping in the shoulders, with definable human features except for a massive projecting ridge of bone above his eyebrows and a prognathic, chinless jaw, a somewhat flattened skull, a low brow; his furred arms just a bit too long and his furred legs just a bit too short for immediately recognizable human symmetry, the feet not entirely arched yet, retaining still a prehensile simian quality, but he was nevertheless a curiously graceful primitive creature and one that was ravenously hungry.

Around nine-thirty that night, Hector Ortega, one of the janitor's staff at the medical school, was trundling his cleaning cart down the basement corridor of B Building, checking doors as he went. The door to the isolation-tank room was unaccountably unlocked. When Ortega went in, he found the lights on. He had never been in this room before; it had been unused for years. The room didn't seem to need cleaning, but he was curious and went in anyway. He looked through the one-way window into the tank room. There was just enough light for Ortega to see an empty room with a black coffinlike contraption in the middle. He thought for a moment that it might be some kind of chapel. He had been working at the medical school for almost six years and had seen all kinds of strange rooms in the basement: physiotherapy rooms and pathology rooms, the morgue and the storage room for the anatomy classes where they hung the cadavers by hooks like sides of beef; why not a chapel? Ortega was a sensible fellow of thirty-nine, and things like cadavers and coffins didn't bother him. At any rate, he opened the door to the tank room to go in for a better look. He had no sooner got the door open when he was bowled off his feet by a hurtling, ferocious little animal, which, in his confusion, Ortega took to be a dog. The suddenness of it certainly frightened him, but only for a few moments. He wasn't about to be frightened of a dog. He muttered a few Spanish curses, scrambled to his feet and went back out into the corridor.

What he saw now, about fifteen yards down the corridor, was an apelike creature the like of which he had never seen before. Not that he knew that much about apes, but he did know they had long arms and matted coarse hair, which this creature didn't have, and apes didn't stand upright on their hind feet like men, as this creature did. It was a small thing, no bigger than Ortega's own nine-year-old son, but it was fierce-looking and was making a threatening, savage, rumbling noise, curling its lip and baring its teeth, which were yellow, even and very human in appearance. By now Ortega was getting scared. He cautiously took hold of his janitor's broom and began unscrewing the long handle. He called out to a colleague whom he had left a corridor away.

"Hey, Jameson!" he called. He called again, louder: "Hey, Jameson! Are you still there? Come here!"

His voice echoed in the empty basement corridors. There was no response. He was frightened by the thought that he would have to deal with this creature alone. Grasping the broom pole in both hands, he took a step toward the strange animal. It watched him carefully. Despite the sloping forehead and the heavy simian brow, the face was much more like a human face than an ape's, and the small, sunken red eyes were measuring him with a human intelligence.

"Hey, Jameson!" Ortega shouted again. "In the name of God, come over here and see this!" He brandished his broom pole at the animal and blurted out in Spanish: "*¡Es mejor que salgas de aquí antes que cometa una locura!*"

The creature's face suddenly flared with rage. It raised both furred fists and screamed in fury. It was too much for Ortega. He turned and bolted down the corridor, wheeled around the corner and raced back toward D Building, where the security office was. Ortega could hear enraged screeches bouncing off the walls behind him. When he got to the security office, he knocked on the door and looked back, clutching his broomstick. The long corridor was deserted but still echoing.

Sergeant George Obispo of the school's security force, a tall, uniformed man, unbolted his door in response to Ortega's knocking. He didn't know Ortega, but he recognized a fellow Puerto Rican. They spoke in Spanish.

"¿Qué pasa?" asked Obispo.

Ortega, who was still breathing hard, took a moment to define for himself just what the matter was. "Hay un animal suelto en el edificio B."

"¿Qué clase de animal es?"

Again, Ortega needed a moment to sort his answer out. "Un mono, yo crea," he said.

From the distant bowels of B Building, the echoing shriek of rage sounded again, caroming off the walls of the empty corridors. "Qué carajo," muttered Sergeant Obispo, and went striding up the corridor, unbuckling his night stick as he went. Ortega trotted along after him, holding his broom pole. Halfway down the corridor, they both pulled up short, because about twenty-five yards in front of them, where their corridor was crossed by the B Building corridor, the strange little creature suddenly loped into view, silhouetted in the diffused yellow light. It paused a moment to regard them and then burst into a shrill bark. It was apparently finding its compressed situation insufferable, trapped as it was by the tight canyon of corridor walls. It moved off abruptly with startling quickness, disappearing into the right half of the B Building corridor.

Obispo and Ortega chugged to the intersection, only to find the B Building corridor empty. There was an exit leading to the street floor at that end of the corridor but its door was heavy and difficult to open, even for a full-grown man. The staff of the medical school had been complaining about it for years. Since it was unlikely the animal knew how to open doors, and even if it did, couldn't have opened this one, they figured they had it cornered. It must have turned into the corridor that debouched to the right and led back to the hospital buildings. That corridor was closed off by a set of doors that were locked after five-thirty in the afternoon.

Sergeant Obispo pulled out his walkie-talkie, strapped to his belt, and made contact with two of his men, who had been assigned that night to guard the library building. "Charlie, we got an animal loose in B Building basement, so you and Mingus come over here right away." He began moving slowly down the corridor to the far end, talking into his walkie-talkie as he went: "We'll be in the north corridor that goes back to the nurses' residence, so you guys come down the other way, and we'll meet you at the door. We'll keep him cornered, but he's a pretty good-sized ape, and I better call the animal rooms and find out what he's doing down here. But be very careful because he looks dangerous. And come in fast because I don't know how long we can hold him down here."

When they got to the north corridor, however, the creature was nowhere to be seen. It was poorly lighted here. One of the overhead fluorescent tubes had blown months ago and had not yet been replaced, another of the regular complaints registered at the janitor's office by the medical school staff. This particular stretch of corridor was a sometime storage area, with a corrugated metal door that led to the Longwood Avenue loading platform on the left side. Several huge empty cardboard cartons stood against the closed metal door. The area was also an auxiliary changing room for the students, and both walls were lined with green and gray lockers. The whole corridor was shrouded in the half shadow of the insufficient lighting.

"He's hiding in there somewhere," suggested Ortega.

"*Yo no se*," said Obispo. He nodded at the exit door. "You think he could've got out that way?"

Ortega didn't think so, but he tugged open the heavy exit door and cautiously leaned in to look up the stairwell to the street floor and down to the subbasement level. Sergeant Obispo, standing at the juncture of the B Building and north corridors, put his walkie-talkie back into its hip case and, holding his club, moved slowly into the shadows between the enfilade of lockers in the north corridor, poking each locker with his club.

Suddenly, with a terrifying shriek, the creature leaped down upon him from the top of the lockers. Obispo fell to the floor with a shout of terror, his club clattering on the cement. Ortega, who had gone halfway down to the subbasement level, came racing back up the stairs, to witness in the distorted shadows of the north corridor, the hideous little creature battering away at the prostrate, screaming Sergeant Obispo with the sergeant's own night stick. Through the wire-reinforced glass windows of the doors thirty yards down, Ortega could see the blurred image of two uniformed security guards ambling toward them from the hospital buildings. At that moment, Obispo's bellows of pain reached them and they broke into a run, pulling out their chains of keys as they came. Security guard Charlie Thomas struggled to unlock the doors. During the few moments it took him to do this, he and his partner, Lew Mingus, had a deformed view of what was going on because of the wire glass in the door windows. What they saw was a confused flux of shadowy shapes on the floor some ten yards away from them, which suddenly exploded into three separate forms. The creature had turned his belligerent attention to Ortega, going after the poor man with a high-pitched scream. Ortega, who had come to Obispo's aid, turned and bolted back down the corridor. Obispo was struggling to his knees. The next thing Thomas and Mingus knew, the rectangular window in the door they were struggling to open was filled with a small, savage, hairy face, made even more horrible by the deforming qualities of the glass. Instinctively they both moved back from the doors, Mingus pulling at his gun holster. Thomas finally got the door open, and the two guards flung themselves into the dark corridor. Sergeant Obispo was still on his knees, a hulking black silhouette, holding his head, which was bleeding badly, and at that moment, he sank unconscious to the floor. Down at the juncture of the corridors, the heavy exit door was slowly wheezing shut. The creature, whatever it was, was gone.

Later on, Jessup remembered little of his scuffle with
Sergeant Obispo and nothing of how he got out of the building. The first clear memory he retained was of rain and
night and the dogs, three scavenger dogs slinking silently
through the wet, dark night, moving past him down the
middle of a dark street. He watched them from some shel-
tered area, perhaps a recessed storefront, but it might have
been one of those burnt-out houses in Roxbury, a ghetto district just southeast of the medical school. Packs of wild dogs
range through Roxbury, especially in the desolated areas.
Jessup watched them pass, and when they had almost disappeared, he slipped out into the rain again and followed
them, loping along, keeping his distance, clutching Sergeant
Obispo's night stick.

He followed the dogs because they made sense to him.
He comprehended dogs; they were familiar to his primitive
consciousness. They were the first familiar, comprehensible
things he had seen that night. Wherever he was, whether in
Roxbury or elsewhere, he must have crossed streets, even
wide and well-traveled avenues, Columbus and Tremont avenues at the least. He must have seen an occasional car,
headlights beaming through the rain, windshield wipers
swishing away. He must have passed houses, lighted windows, the peripheral sound of television, the other noises of
the city. He probably saw a pedestrian or two. But he remembered nothing of cars, houses or pedestrians. These
things were utterly beyond his comprehension, and no impression of them was retained. He knew only that he was
alone and isloated in alien terrain, and that he was impelled
by the most primal instincts, to live through the night, to

find food, water, to avoid predators, to survive. Anything more than that he did not recognize or remember.

He followed the dogs because, like himself, they were silent, solemn hunters, hungry, lean, dangerous animals. They sniffed at metal trash cans and mauled plastic garbage bags. He remembered they crossed an expanse of flat ground, filled with a kind of scree and stones, probably one of the areas in lower Roxbury that have been demolished. He followed along some fifty yards behind the dogs, pausing in this area to pick up a jagged stone. Later on, when it was all over, he was still holding the stone. In point of fact, it was a piece of broken red brick. The dogs crossed the rubble, with Jessup trailing them like an animal who hadn't been accepted into the pack yet. A strange, savage, surreal scene in the derelict heart of the city, three wild dogs and a small apelike creature, slinking silently through the glistening, black, empty streets, hunting for prey.

The dogs knew where they were going, of course. This was their territory. They were headed for the Van Buren Park Zoo. There was a hole in the fence they knew, and once inside the park, they preyed on sleeping wildfowl and small animals. First, they marauded some garbage cans in front of the row of small apartment houses that faced on the zoo. They sniffed up a couple of alleys and down some basement steps. They were looking for rats. Jessup stood in the rain, his fine fur soaked through, holding his club and his stone, watching the dogs from a safe distance. He was hearing familiar sounds now, the trills and croaks of birds just on the other side of the high iron fence. He waited patiently, mutely, a small, not very formidable furred creature with the brain capacity of a gorilla but with the genetic cunning to recognize the value of a stone and a club.

There was a small, snarling flurry across the wet street as the dogs threatened each other over something they had found. It couldn't have been much. The savage little fight was over in a few seconds. The dogs slunk back across the street to the zoo side, wet, filthy, hyena-like animals. They moved farther on, sniffing, poking about with their muzzles at the foot of the fence. Jessup watched them without moving a muscle, tense, alert. He knew he was in the dogs' wind. One of them suddenly wheeled toward him, its yellow eyes wide and its lip drawn back, exposing the teeth. In a fraction of a second, the other dogs as well were snarling softly at Jessup. He wasn't frightened. He knew these animals. With a shrill shriek, he dashed at the dogs, brandishing his stick and stone. The dogs slunk back, keeping their distance. His shriek aroused the birds in the zoo park. There was a sudden fluttering of distant wings and birds calling danger to their fellows. Two of the dogs were obviously waiting for the leader to do something. The lead dog, a mongrel mastiff with white markings on its brow, padded, growling softly, into the street, moving to Jessup's flank. Jessup watched him warily. He snarled threateningly at the dog. He snarled again. Then, suddenly, the mongrel attacked, leaping for Jessup's throat. Jessup battered at the glistening, red-tongued maw of the dog's mouth. The other two dogs lunged in. Jessup faced them with fury, screaming his anger into the rain and darkness, smashing at the dogs with his club and piece of stone.

Then something happened which Jessup could not remember clearly. The feral little mortal struggle was somehow interrupted, possibly by a passing car. The approaching roar of a motor and the sweeping headlights may have sent the three dogs scuttling off. When they returned to resume the battle, they found Jessup perched on the stonework that formed the top of the zoo fence. Here he squatted and, apelike, taunted the three dogs below. He tired of that after a few moments and clambered down the other side into the zoo. He suddenly found himself on ground and grass. The zoo itself was not lighted at night, but there was enough of a spill from the streetlights for Jessup to see bushes and trees glistening in the rain. He was in familiar terrain again, and he grunted with pleasure.

He was in the pheasants' area, a field that sloped up to the wildfowl pond. In the thin light he could see the low wattled fence and the wet grass quickly receding upward into blackness and silence. The zoo was asleep, hushed. It was perhaps eleven o'clock. After a moment, he thought he caught a faint glow of red on the crest of the slope, and he thought he heard the distant burr of a crane. He shuffled forward through the wet grass, and found himself on one of the walkways that wind through the park, and proceeded for a few moments until he saw a small body of water, the wildfowl pond, glistening blackly in the night. The rain had slackened now to a misty drizzle. It was a warm night for April. The air hung heavy and fetid with the smell of animals, silent with a massive sensation of sleep.

The total blackness and silence bothered Jessup; it was not quite right. He was desperately thirsty and considered climbing the small fence that surrounded the pond and slaking his thirst, but he still didn't trust this terrain. He followed the pathway to the left around the fence. He didn't like the feel of the wet macadam beneath him, but it was clearly a pathway, cutting between dripping trees and bushes against which he brushed now and then. He was suddenly in an open area and startled by the abrupt rearing up of a stone building, faintly visible only by the relative lightness in color of the stone against the darkness of the night.

He was some hundred yards into the zoo now, and only the last tracings of light from the outside street reached here, reflecting weakly off the windows of the building. Jessup didn't know what to make of the building. He moved on, sensing his way. Again he saw the red glow, this time off to his right, and he slipped softly in that direction. What he was seeing were the night lights of a building which glowed red because of the tinting of the windows and the glass of the doors. When he approached this long, low stone building, rising in a soft red haze out of the night, he was fascinated. He moved cautiously across the plaza of the building to the front doors and peered into the interior. He saw a long empty hall bathed in a red light that showed rows of cages on each side. In the cages were mice, porcupines, sloths and shrews, curled up in balls of sleep, with an occasional movement here and there as one of the small animals slithered across its cage to its watering trough. It was all as incomprehensible to Jessup as a television set to a cat. Uncomprehending, he was quickly bored.

He moved on farther into the hushed blackness of the zoo, making his way around large round empty cages with thick iron bars, down macadam paths lined by protective iron railings. Again he heard the croaking burr of a crane, much closer now. He stopped short, froze, waited, listened. To his left, a large stone outcropping rose, barely discernible; directly ahead was a round, iron-fenced area. On his right, suddenly, behind the fence of wooden wattles, he sensed movement, and then a crowned crane moved stiffly into his vision, its gray body nearly invisible in the darkness, though the glistening red and white spots on its face and the stiff, large, straw-colored topknot of feathers on its head were recognizable in the red glow. It stood a moment, staring blankly out of its button eyes, then turned and disappeared into the darkness. Jessup stood unmoving, holding his broken bit of brick tightly, considering the possibility of killing the bird. He was riven with hunger. But everything was all too strange here. He didn't understand the stone buildings, the red glow, the transparency of the windows, the iron fences, the wattled palisades. He padded softly up to the low wooden fence and peered into the darkness, trying to see the crane again, but it was gone. He moved on.

Then he was home. It was impenetrably dark, but he knew he was home. He could hear the sounds of the East African grasslands in front of him, the movement of animals, the sudden, startled flurry of veering herds, antelope, he suspected. He felt a thick bramble in front of him. He raised a protective forearm against it, brushed the branches away. It was actually a four-foot-high hedgerow disguising a wooden fence that enclosed the section of the park known as the African Plains. He forced his way through the hedge, crawled between the horizontal poles of the fence and found himself on grass again, on the edge of a shallow moat about four feet deep and ten feet wide. Once again, there was a sufficient spill of light from the street outside to afford Jessup about the same range of vision he would have had on an ordinary moonlit night. He was on high ground, and a tract of savanna stretched out before him, dark and silent, misty in the drizzle. Far down to his left, he could see the glisten of a water hole. On his right, a slight slope of sparse woodland and a sleeping group of blesboks, perhaps three of them. He grunted with pleasure.

He let himself down into the moat, which was as deep as he was tall. It was utterly black in here. He had to walk along it a number of yards before he found an overhanging limb by which he could pull himself up to the other side. When he clambered up out of the moat, he was on a small stone outcrop, and his appearance startled a herd of perhaps forty Thomson's gazelles that were huddled for the night near the wooden palisade of their paddock. In a moment, the whole herd of skittish, tiny antelopes was up and slewing madly out into the open grass. Jessup held his bit of brick, ready to kill. He stood stock still, patiently waiting to become part of this world, waiting for his presence, his smell, his movements, to become familiar, natural, rooted. The night became silent again. Peripherally, he could see the water hole about thirty yards to his left and what seemed to be a single hartebeest humped forward, lapping quietly at the water. He moved silently through the wet grass, heading for the end of the water hole farthest from the hartebeest. He didn't want to startle the animal. He just wanted to drink. Then he would kill something and eat, not the hartebeest, this large antelope was far too big for him to kill alone, it would have to be one of the little gazelles. He stood at the edge of the water hole, trying to sense the presence of predators other than himself; there were none. The hartebeest across the water hole had raised its head and was watching him, ready to bolt. Jessup got down slowly on both knees, bent forward and began to lap the water. After a moment, the hartebeest returned to its own drinking. For a moment, the two animals shared the water hole, each drinking silently, warily.

Even as he drank, he planned his kill. He understood the hunting of antelopes; he had hunted them before. But never alone, only in packs. His kind always hunted in packs, fanning out through the high grass, cunning little carnivores capable of killing elephants, giant goats, antelopes five times the size of any one of them; ravening, grunting little brutes, slow of foot, clumsy at climbing, but peerless hunters with their clubs and sticks and sharp stones. But because he was alone, it would have to be the miniature gazelles, the small herd of which was now sleeping in the sparse little grove of trees on a slope about fifty yards off. Edgy animals, there were always a skittish few wandering on the periphery of the flock, flicking here and there like butterflies. He could never catch one in the open; they were much too fleet. He would have to isolate one and herd it against the pale of the paddock, or possibly drive it into the moat. Once in the moat he could get it.

Finished drinking, he carefully got back on his feet and slipped slowly off toward the slope where the Thomson's gazelles huddled, trembling even as they slept. There was no cover of high grass under which to approach. He would have to let the gazelles accustom themselves to his presence if he was to get close to them at all. When he was about thirty yards away, he squatted and stayed put. He studied the land around him. The zoo slept. Nothing moved anywhere. The air was heavy and wet, but the rain itself had stopped. He waited. A flicker of movement in the antelope herd. A fawn leaped and bounded this way and that and rejoined the herd. Abruptly, three gazelles leaped, ran, whirled, hardly more than fluttering shadows of movement. He rose from his squat, slowly, cautiously, so as not to frighten the animals, turned his back on them, moved slowly away. He was looking for stones now, a clod of earth, a small, heavy piece of wood, anything he could throw. He headed for a clump of trees. There was always something around trees, hardened animal droppings perhaps, which is just what he found. He picked up two pieces and unobtrusively made his way back to within twenty yards of the antelope herd. Holding his club and his stone in one hand, he pitched the two pieces into the trees where the herd lay, legs folded beneath them in shallow sleep. With the first rustle of leaves, the herd exploded dementedly, racing, leaping, scattering like leaves caught in a swirl of wind. Half a dozen leaped and skittered wildly past Jessup. He was after them with a shriek, driving their agitated, mad shadows before him past the water hole, straight for the moat. At the lip of the moat, all but one veered and shot off into darkness. The one tried to leap the chasm. It was too much for the tiny animal. It fell in a heap to the bottom of the moat, crippled. Grunting at his success, Jessup jumped into the moat and with one stroke of his club smashed in the animal's skull.

He began scraping away at its hide with his jagged chip of brick. He had stripped a good piece off one of the antelope's haunches when he sensed danger. He stood, waited. Then he heard it, a low growl. He picked up his kill by a leg and moved softly, quickly, up the wide, dark moat. The sides were just high enough to obscure his vision. He needed to get out of the moat. He was looking for an overhanging branch, anything he could pull himself up with. He finally found one. He put the antelope carcass on the lip of the moat and hauled himself up beside it. He stood silently, looking around the wet dark terrain. He was high on the slope again and could make out the crowns of a few trees above him and the water hole down below. He could see nothing else. He could hear nothing else. He squatted down, his rump grazing the wet black grass. He transferred his chip of brick to his club hand, and with his free hand, he raised the antelope carcass to his face, clamping his teeth into the hot, wet, bloody flesh. He twisted his head back and forth, wrenching the gobbet of flesh free, and chewed at it.

Then he saw the three dogs moving up the slope from the water hole, smallish lumps of black movement in the black grass. In a moment, they were close enough for him to recognize the white markings on the mastiff's brow. Still squatting, Jessup snarled at them, brandished his club. The dogs skulked back into the grass. He wasn't afraid of the dogs. He knew they wanted his kill, not him. He buried his face in the antelope's haunch again and wrenched off another gob of meat. The dogs skulked forward. He waved his club at them. They skulked back. That was the last he remembered, squatting in the slope in the wet grass, eating the antelope in the night with a great, sullen satisfaction, occasionally warding off the snarling dogs with a snarl of his own, a threatening wave of his club, a primal animal at one with his elemental world.

A little after 2 A.M., the guard on patrol duty at the zoo that night thought he saw some movement on the African Plains. He stopped his car, got out, leaned over the hedgerow and peered into the darkness. There was certainly something going on, a lot of low snarling and growling. He walked around the hedgerow to where it turned into a Rotterdam fence, a tilted wire barrier that prevented the animals from getting out but was easily slipped over by a man. The moon was out now, and he could see pretty well what was going on. It was three dogs ravening something in the grass. The guard drew his gun and climbed the fence. The dogs saw him immediately and raced away. He walked nervously over to see what they had been tearing at. It was the remains of a Thomson's gazelle. The guard turned quickly because he felt sick, and he would have headed back to his car, but his eye was caught by a large blur of white in the darkness beneath a tree about twenty yards away. He cocked his revolver and edged slowly in that direction. It was the body of a naked man. At first, the guard thought it was a dead man, but then he saw the even rise and fall of the man's chest. The guard was struck by what could only be called a beatific smile on the sleeping man's face.

Jessup was awakened, taken to the zoo's security office, given a raincoat to cover his nakedness, and then brought to the Van Buren Park precinct station, where he was booked. The police took it for granted that he was a mental case, and Jessup, as the better part of valor, did nothing to dissuade them. They did, however, at his request, call his wife, who said she would be down straightaway. Emily dressed quickly, jeans, sweater and a jacket, and woke her landlady, who agreed to baby-sit during this emergency. Because she was simply too distraught to be alone, she called Mason Parrish, who picked her up twenty minutes later and drove her to the precinct house. Jessup, wearing the borrowed raincoat, was brought out of the lockup.

"I've brought you some pants and a sweater," said Parrish.

"Thank you," murmured Jessup. "See what you can do about getting me out of here."

The police were only too glad to turn Jessup over to his wife. They were out of the station in fifteen minutes. While he was climbing into Parrish's car, Jessup said, "I'd like to stop by the medical school. I left all my clothes in the tank room."

"Let's just get you home," said Emily, sliding into the front seat on his right. "It's three-thirty in the morning."

"I have my watch and my wallet there. My keys are there. I'll need them to get in the apartment."

"I've still got mine," said Emily.

Parrish slid behind the wheel, shut his door. "I'll go back and get your clothes for you later."

Parrish turned over the motor and they moved out into the empty dark street.

Jessup seemed in a state of shock, distracted by distant thoughts, oddly placid, stunned, lobotomized. He sat sandwiched between his wife and Parrish, staring through the windshield, almost unaware of their presence.

"What were you doing in the tank room?" she asked. He didn't seem to hear her. "Do you remember anything at all about last night?"

He stared at her blankly, murmured, "I remember large fragments of what happened, but not all of it. You'll have to be patient with me." He turned back into his thoughts.

"I had Mason and Arthur running all over Boston looking for you all night," she said. She let her face sink onto his chest, and she wept. She heard his voice muttering into her hair, "It's okay. Really, I'm fine." It seemed incredible to her that she had arrived back from Africa only a little more than twelve hours before.

Parrish dropped them off at the red-brick building on Powell Street that they had shared for seven years. Emily went up the stoop to the ivy-framed door, unlocked it, and Jessup followed her down the hallway to his apartment. She flicked on the living room lights and they went in.

"It's a good deal tidier than when I was living here," she said. "I want to call home to see if the kids are okay."

"I'm going to take a shower," he said. It was as if they had come home from the theater.

She was in the kitchen having cookies and coffee when he came out fifteen minutes later, swathed in a towel-robe, patting himself dry. He made himself a cup of instant coffee. He seemed in a very good mood. He smiled.

"I suppose," he said, "getting a call from the police at three o'clock in the morning to the effect that your husband has been found sleeping naked in the Van Buren Park Zoo might have caused you some concern."

"Yes, I think you could say that."

"And Mason's been writing you all this time telling you I'm having a nervous breakdown, and you figured I finally flipped out altogether." He put his cup on the table, sat down across from her and would have said something, but he began to laugh. It was a full, open laugh. "I'm sorry, Emily, forgive me," he said when he could. "I know what an absolutely harrowing day I've been giving you. I'm sure you've been sitting here all this while trying to figure out how to convince me to see a psychiatrist."

"As a matter of fact, I have."

"I don't know how you've put up with me all these years."

"I loved you."

She wasn't put out by his high spirits. She was pleased, in fact, to see this sudden and uncharacteristic exuberance. Exuberant was the only word she could apply to his behavior at that moment. His cheeks were flushed and steamed from the shower, his eyes glinted with pleasure. He beamed at her over his coffee cup. She found herself smiling back. In a moment, some deep inner exhilaration engulfed him, and he had to set the cup down for fear of spilling the coffee. He stood, crying out in exultation: "Oh, my God, Emily! I don't know how to tell you this! I really don't!" He stared at her, exalted with the cosmic comedy of it all. "Oh, my God, Emily, bear with me! The implications are staggering!"

He went into the living room, where he moved erratically around the room, motored by an uncontrolled energy. She followed him, standing in the kitchen doorway, watching him. He said, "I don't remember all of it. Apparently, I entered a very primitive consciousness, and all I can remember of last night was what was comprehensible to that consciousness. I don't remember, at least not clearly, how I got out of the tank room. The first thing I remember are the dogs. I remember the dogs very well."

He sat on the arm of the overstuffed chair. She stayed in the doorway. "On a strictly physiological level," he said, "I suspect the drug we've been using achieved an observable momentum at enough nuclear locations to alter the actual form. It probably affects the bonding. What we need is some tissue specimens, get a biophysicist to run some electron-spin resonance tests. What they do is pulse some cells through an energy range, and when they pass through the right energy band, the electron spins flip. My guess is the carbonyls, which are normally inactive, became free radicals, or at least free to create the radicals which would allow an orderly breakdown of the cell and alter the activity of the proteins. But suppose we could establish a biochemical setting for this singular event; so what? Suppose we get some cells, crack them open, get some assays. Okay, so we get all kinds of whacked-out polyribosomal profiles. I'm loaded with monster ribosomes. Fantastic enzymatic activity. All the polymerases are labeling phenomenally high. I'm making protein at an unbelievable pace. I mean, let's face it!

This whole thing is biologically impossible! We're not just talking about one cell or even a colony of cells going wild. This isn't an instance of cancerous hypertrophy. We're talking about every one of the trillions of cells in my body changing all at the same time, a massive mutation of my entire biological system, a process that took millions of years to evolve reversing itself in a matter of hours, if not moments! I could've exploded and blown up half of Boston with me! Biologically, it is simply impossible!"

He had been all over the room during this discourse. Now he turned to Emily with a smile of delight forming on his face. "So we'll have to go outside biology to understand this. We'll have to go to disciplines that do not necessarily regard time and space as linear dimensions. We'll have to go to the physicists. Some extraordinary transfer of energy has occurred, sort of a radioactive thing. Don't we have a physicist in our circle of friends? Parrish knows a whole bunch of those flakes out at MIT. I'd like to bounce this off a quantum guy. Because you see, Emily, what I think happened is I somehow got into a quantum state where there is no matter, only the potential of matter." He sat slowly back on the arm of the soft chair. He muttered, "Yes. It makes sense, doesn't it? Some original and universal state of energy potential. I somehow tapped into that original consciousness of pure potential. My God, what an implacably beautiful thought!"

He stood up slowly, literally glowing, radiant with creativity, one of those moments in which the mists lift and all the horizons of the world are visible and clear as crystal. He stood stock still in the middle of the room, closed his eyes

and stared into eternity. His face was as masklike as an
icon's. He muttered, "It must be true. Anything that beautiful must be true." All Emily could think about was how extraordinarily sensual he seemed; she was watching a man in
the transports of love.

"We might be able to localize this force of consciousness in one tissue, in one cell even," he speculated.
"We could determine its effect on other organisms. That's
what that son of a bitch at the U of M has been trying to do
for fifteen years. He's picked up on all Burr's stuff. Burr's the
guy who did all that work on life fields at Yale. What he's
working on now is trying to change L-fields through manipulation of consciousness. But I'll beat that son of a bitch to
Stockholm yet! Tonight I jumped a million years ahead of
him!" He stared at Emily, eyes glistening with exultancy. He
cried out, "I tell you, Emily, I think I've found the Ultimate
Force! I've found the Final Truth! I found it, and I can
bring it into a laboratory and demonstrably quantify it!"

He sighed as if in consummation and sank back into the
embrace of the soft chair, ravished.

"I don't understand a thing you're talking about," said
Emily, who was beginning to be a little frightened again.

He lay sprawled in the soft chair. He seemed almost to
be asleep. He murmured: "After I left you this afternoon, I
went to the isolation-tank room, took two hundred milligrams of the stuff, got into the tank, programmed myself
into my own original life force, and at some point during the
evening, I physically transformed my matter into some form
of early human life, perhaps the earliest."

She straightened her hair nervously. "What do you mean, you transformed yourself?"

"I turned into a small, finely furred, erect, bipedal, protohuman creature. I followed a pack of wild dogs to the zoo. That's how I got there. They attacked me, and I climbed into the zoo to get away from them. In the zoo, I hunted down, killed and ate a small gazelle. I was utterly primal. I consisted of nothing more than the will to survive, to live through the night, to eat, to drink, to sleep. It was the most supremely satisfying time of my life. I was at one with my world, with all the forces of life around me, an instance of energy in a total symmetry. I experienced the primal unity. I was my true self. I remember everything of last night that relates to that self. I cannot remember anything else. I cannot, as I say, remember how I got out of the isolation-tank room or out of the medical school buildings or what happened to me before I saw the dogs."

The doorbell rang.

"That must be Mason," she said, grateful for the interruption.

"Look, Emily, I don't expect you to believe me. If someone told me a story like this, I'd think he was crazy too. But I know it happened, so I have to believe it. The thing to do is to do it again, and you can observe it, you and Arthur and Mason, all responsible scientists. I can't repeat the experiment again for two weeks because of the rapid tolerance, but we can use the two weeks to very good purpose. There's a lot of tests that will have to be prepared. We should certainly take film of the event if it happens. We should take tissue and blood samples. I'd like to talk to some physicists, some molecular biologists, because, frankly, I can't explain how or why it happened. All I'm asking of you is to come and see if it happens again before you categorically dismiss me as a madman. That doesn't seem very much to ask."

The bell rang again. She stood and started for the door.

"I may have killed a man tonight," he said, "or damn near killed him. I remember beating somebody bloody."

She paused briefly at the door, sighed, then opened it. Parrish boomed into the room, carrying Jessup's clothing over his arm. "Man!" he announced. "You don't know the trouble I had getting these clothes! I had to go to the security office for them! They want you to call them right now. There was some kind of ape in your isolation-tank room tonight; do you know anything about that? This ape almost killed a security guard. You didn't bring an ape down to the tank room tonight, did you? Your watch and stuff are in the jacket pocket." He could see from the silence that something was wrong. He smiled nervously at Emily. "Is everything all right? Is he okay?"

She looked up briefly, stood and went to the kitchen to get more coffee, saying as she went, "If he's okay, the rest of us are in a lot of trouble." At the kitchen doorway, she suggested to her husband, "Tell Mason what you've been telling me. I'd like to hear Mason's views on all this."

"I think Mason's views will be predictable," said Jessup.

Cambridge, Harvard
Medical School
April–May 1976

And, of course, Mason's views were predictable. Some things were simply inadmissible, at least in the orderly universe Parrish wished to inhabit. There was a far more sensible explanation for Jessup's ridiculous episode that night: he had finally exceeded his tolerance of the hallucinogens he had been taking, and he had simply freaked out, zoned out, had a toxic delirium. Such irrational behavior—running naked around the streets of Boston and going to sleep in the city zoo—was not the first or the worst instance of drug-induced breakdown that Parrish had heard of. A guy he had known in med school had dropped a little too much acid and jumped out of a twelfth-story window. What worried Parrish was that Jessup actually believed his hallucination, that he couldn't tell hallucination from reality anymore. That was scary, that was sick, and he thought Jessup ought to see somebody about that. As for the belligerent ape in the basement of the Harvard Medical School, Parrish was sure that it would turn out to be one of the local kids who had broken into the school, looking to pinch some equipment or drugs or something equally undramatic.

In any event, Parrish snorted out his disbelief of Jessup's tale of transmogrification, and Emily was grateful for it. For one brief moment, when Parrish had come barreling into the room with his news about the wayward ape, she had experienced a swift, dizzying feeling of disintegration; that is to say, for one brief moment she had almost believed her husband, and it was good to hear Parrish's relentless sanity.

Jessup was insufferably sensible about their disbelief. "Look, you people think I had a toxic delirium," he said to them. "Okay. I understand that. So let's find out. There's only one way to find out. Let's try it again. If I flip out, you can always bring me down with a little benzodiazepine, if that's all you're worried about."

"What I'm worried about," shouted Parrish, "is you've got a couple of grams of that shit in you, you've obviously transcended your tolerance of it, and you don't know what damage you're doing to yourself!"

"Oh, Mason, come on, if I've stacked up so much of that drug, an increment of another two hundred milligrams isn't going to make or break me. The point is, I don't think it was a toxic delirium. I think it really happened, and there's only one way to find out, and that's to try it again and you people observe it."

Just before five that morning, Mrs. Lindsay called to say Margaret, the younger child, had awakened, was uncontrollably cranky and was demanding her mother, so Emily left to take care of that. The rest of the weekend continued to be a nightmare for Emily. She hadn't had more than a few hours' sleep since she left Africa two days before, and she wasn't about to get much more that morning, what with the house a holy mess and both the kids, sensing the unspoken hysteria, in sour moods. She had made arrangements with Mrs. Thorpe, her old housekeeper, to come by that morning to help her get organized in her new home, but that wasn't till ten-thirty, and by the time Mrs. Thorpe showed up, it was all Emily could do to fall fully clothed on her mattress and sink into a fretful sleep. She awoke at two in the afternoon in panic, scrambled to the telephone and called Jessup, but there was no answer. She called Parrish, who said Jessup was probably at the Harvard Coop picking up books on theoretical physics; at least, that was what he had said he was going to do when Parrish left him at daybreak. Emily thought she and Parrish and Rosenberg should get together and talk about what to do about all this. Then she remembered that the Rosenbergs had said something about visiting family in Providence that day. So it wasn't till Sunday afternoon that the Rosenbergs and Parrish came over, and they sat around the cluttered living room discussing Jessup.

It was the first the Rosenbergs had heard of Jessup's eventful night in the zoo. Rosenberg thought Jessup's explanation of that night improbable and tended to agree with the others that it had more likely been a psychedelic episode. On the other hand, he said, Jessup had been right in saying another two hundred milligrams of the drug wouldn't be critical. Rosenberg had no objection to observing Jessup do it again in two weeks. Emily disagreed; she thought they should do everything they could to dissuade him from continuing his experiment, but even Parrish thought that futile.

"There is no way nohow you're going to talk him out of going into that tank again," he said to Emily. "You know him better than I do, and you know he's going to do it, with us or without us. As a matter of fact, it'd be better if we were there."

Then, suddenly, it was Monday, and the nightmarish incidents of Friday night seemed remote, talked out, overdiscussed. Parrish and Rosenberg were back in their classrooms and laboratories, and Jessup had his nine o'clock class in Physiology 1. And Emily awoke that Monday morning at six-thirty, made breakfast for herself and the kids, got them washed and dressed, spent the morning getting them into a school for faculty children and then began shopping for window shades. At noon, Mrs. Thorpe arrived at the house, and they finished the unpacking. Emily busied herself furiously with all this domesticity until in a quiet moment, while Mrs. Thorpe was fixing dinner for them all, she went to the phone and called Jessup again. She had spoken to him late Saturday night and again on Sunday morning, and he had seemed fine then, and he certainly seemed fine now.

He had bought some books on quantum mechanics and

was boning up on it so that when he got around to talking with some physicists, he would have at least a little grounding in the subject. By now it was apparently taken for granted that she, Parrish and Rosenberg would all come down to the isolation-tank room a week from Friday and observe him in the tank. In fact, a number of tests had been planned in case the transmogrification actually did occur. Emily was a little unnerved by how quickly the transmogrification had become a possibility. She reminded Jessup he really should allow a little time for the children. He hadn't seen them in a year, and they were asking about him. She suggested she bring them over to his place on an afternoon after they got out of school, and he could take them someplace, she almost said the zoo. That would give her a chance to have a look at all his data, listen to his tapes, study his reports. She wanted to bring herself up to date on what had been going on this past year. Jessup thought that a marvelous idea and suggested Thursday because he had an afternoon class on Tuesday and he and Parrish were going over to MIT on Wednesday to talk to some physicists.

The data that most impressed Emily that Thursday afternoon were the blood analyses from the Goodman and the Sarich labs. There was always the possibility of technical error in any lab test, but hardly from two separate and reputable laboratories such as these. There was little doubt that some curious genetic change, however transitory, had occurred. Rosenberg's reports on the fractionating of the drug mixture went right by her. Chemistry was her weakest point. And the x-rays taken of Jessup's throat looked simian, but it had been some time since she had examined an x-ray, and she didn't think these were all that clear anyway. But the tapes of Jessup's experiences in the tank, especially the one during which his aphasic instance occurred, fascinated her. The vocalizations he had made on that tape were startlingly similar to the baboon vocalizations she had just recorded in Africa. Nor were the dramatic effects of the tape lost on her. By the time she had put all the stuff back in Jessup's filing cabinet, she found herself stimulated and excited and curious in that special way in which scientists get curious.

They all went to a McDonald's for dinner, a typical American family in a large dining room of typical American families, except that this mother kept pressing this father to recall every detail he could of an experience he had had perhaps eight or ten million years ago. The kids were enchanted by their father's fanciful story. The dinner passed pleasantly. Jessup also told her about his lunch with the physicists at MIT the previous day. He was unusually relaxed and made it all sound very amusing.

Parrish had set up the lunch with a quantum mechanician pal of his, who, he alerted Jessup, was a screwball even for a quantum mechanician. "They're all certifiable at MIT, you know, all of them," Parrish briefed Jessup. "You spend ten minutes with some of these high-energy-physics guys, and you're in never-never land. You've got to hang ballast on those guys, or they'd zip off to the moon. I once met a mathematician out there, I asked him what he was working on, he said he was breeding mathematical theorems to produce a superior breed of mathematical theorems! I mean, you're talking to certifiable lunatics out there!"

Parrish's friend's name was Willard Sproule, who proved to be a very likable young fellow of thirty-odd years, but what with his John Denver haircut and wire-rimmed glasses and open sport shirt, he looked hardly twenty. His eyes were continually blinking behind his glasses, and he seemed to be constantly smiling in expectation of something wondrous to happen. Everything elicited an "Oh, wow!" from him, even the simple act of being introduced to Jessup. The lunch had started in the cafeteria at MIT and had continued as they ambled across the paths of the campus to Sproule's office, accreting scientists along the way. By the time they got to Sproule's office, there was a biophysicist named Goddard, a theoretical physicist named Murdoch, and a molecular biologist named Garrett Durrell, all of whom turned out to be—in Parrish's muttered opinion— thoroughly accredited flakes. None of them seemed to think the idea of a man turning into an ape off the wall at all, at least not beyond the scope of speculation. All of them said that if Jessup intended to repeat this singular feat, they would certainly like to watch. Jessup thought about that for a moment but finally decided against it. It might have been only a particularly vivid hallucinatory experience, and he didn't want to expose himself to the ridicule of the scientific community, at least not till he had gathered a more considerable body of hard evidence. At this stage, he preferred to keep it on a strictly speculative level, a brainstorming session for the fun of it. The MIT flakes promptly accommodated. There were times in Sproule's office when neither Jessup nor Parrish could make out a word, what with everybody shouting at the same time, one or another of them leaping up to seize a piece of chalk to give impromptu lectures on the blackboard.

The physicists saw the whole thing in terms of particles and energy states. Goddard suggested that Jessup might have succeeded in effecting slight alterations in his energy states, facilitating certain electron exchanges, creating, as it were, a sort of primordial soup of proteins, which would then tend to recombine at the nearest preferred energy level. You do get situations in particle physics, and for that matter in the Bermuda Triangle, for all Goddard knew, where you have something in one state and then suddenly you'll find it appearing in another state. It has apparently zipped through a forbidden region between the states. That sort of decay has been observed often enough in particle interaction. What Jessup may have accomplished, granted the veracity of his story, was to have managed to reduce his uncertainty in energy to zero or near enough to zero so that the time available to him to tunnel through had been infinite. He had somehow controlled the energy of all his elemental particles simultaneously. But how had he somehow done this? What triggered it?

Here even the physicists were divided. Sproule saw the whole thing as an instance of wave-packet reduction. Murdoch was a theoretical physicist, more of a mathematician really, and what fascinated him was that Jessup had somehow managed to revisit his past. He could think of several explanations for this, but the one he fancied most was that Jessup had somehow got into a Gödel time trajectory. Gödel, a colleague of Einstein's, had conceived of time not so much as a dimension but as huge closed rings, the smallest radius of which was the radius of the universe. "If I just take a little bunch of particles in a certain region of space-time," Murdoch explained, "and suck them up, I can explain in a Gödel universe why somebody returns to the same time and structure. There are certain curves—if you go along the same time line—strictly controlled by the acceleration in space-time. If you have the same amount of energy and it's held constant, you would have to come back to the same event. But you'd need a fantastic amount of acceleration, I mean, absolutely fantastic." The problem with the Gödel universe thing, of course, as Sproule pointed out, was that when Jessup had been roving around Boston in his protohuman state, he would have perforce sucked all Boston into his own space-time. This, of course, hadn't happened.

Jessup, who relished speculation for its own sake as well as the next man, had enjoyed the afternoon. He admitted to Emily now that the physicists and he had different concepts of consciousness. They thought of it as a particular force exerted by a particular person. Jessup saw consciousness as a cosmic, perhaps *the* cosmic force. This universe of ours had exploded into being some twenty billion years ago, a fantastic explosion of hydrogen, and it was still exploding past us at ninety million miles an hour. So there had been a beginning, and there would be an end. Okay, what came before and what comes after? Where did that original hydrogen come from? You could call it a divine act of creation if you liked, said Jessup, but he preferred to think our universe was the other end of a black hole of a previous universe. In short, there was a prior force that exploded the original hydrogen, that conceived the other forces of nature, nuclear, gravitational and electromagnetic. Forces don't create themselves; they have to be created. This original creative force was what Jessup considered consciousness. You could call it God if you wanted to, but there was a difference. Consciousness was not a noumenal or a spiritual process; it was phenomenologically available; it could be reached, tapped into, manipulated; Lord knows, Jessup believed he had demonstrably tapped into it. How he had tapped into it he hadn't the faintest clue. There were so many variables.

The dinner, a leisurely one, lasted till both kids had their heads on the table. Jessup saw them all back to Cambridge. He was still in the best of spirits, and there was a tenuous moment when he suggested he stay the night; but Emily made it clear she thought that would be foolish. She had just spent a year separating herself from Jessup, only to have her suppressed feelings ripped open and exposed by the events of the last weekend, and she wasn't happy to learn that she was still so susceptible to him. She thought she had made her peace with the idea of divorce, had even begun saying things like it could well be the best thing that had happened to her. She was determined to keep the separation unmuddled by sex.

She sent him back to his flat and then turned off the lights and sat in the dark living room and let herself sink into a wretchedness mixed with outrage, outrage at Jessup for having savaged her feelings, outrage at herself for letting him do it so easily. But there was more to this wounded mood than that. She could feel a menacing sensation of hysteria insinuating through her raw feelings, and finally, by an

effort of will, she recognized the hysteria as fear. She tried
to define the fear, but her mind, normally disciplined,
resisted, balked. She was manifestly afraid of the fear. She
went to sleep with it, indeed she went to sleep to escape it,
and lying there on the simple mattress and box spring and
thinking she really ought to buy a bed frame, she didn't like
sleeping this low to the floor, the fear suddenly penetrated
her, visible, identifiable, and she recognized what it was.
She was afraid that Jessup's grotesque, demented, incredible
story of having changed for a brief period into a hominid
creature might be true, and that, God save her, she was beginning to believe him, that she had, in fact, probably
believed him from the first.

There was no sleep for her now. She got up and roamed
through the dark rooms of her flat, pausing in the doorway
of the kids' room, watching them sleep, telling herself this
was just one of those midnight panics and everything would
make sense again in the morning. But she knew it wouldn't,
that something terrible was happening and that she must
deal with it. It was not yet one o'clock, so she called Jessup.
"I'm in a kind of wild panic, Eddie. I need to talk to you."

"I'll be right over," he said.

She watched from the porch window as he pulled up to
the house and went to the door to let him in. He was no
sooner into the darkness of the foyer than she said, "I don't
know how even to put this into words, but I'm beginning to
think that what happened to you last Friday night was not
just a hallucinatory experience. I've got this gut feeling
something phenomenological did actually happen, that
there was some kind of genetic transformation. I don't know

why I think that in defiance of all rationality, but I do. And now that I do, I'm terrified, I mean, really terrified, petrified."

"So am I," he said.

They moved to the threshold of the living room, where they paused again in the periphery of the lamplight.

"I don't want you doing this experiment again next week," she said.

"We've got to find out if it actually happened, Emily."

"I'm suggesting that you put it off until we understand a little more of what might have happened and so minimize the risk."

"There is no way we can understand this before the event," he said. "It's an inexplicable singularity, and we can only work back from the event itself. We have to know it happened; then we can work back to try to understand how and why it happened."

"You don't understand what I'm saying."

"I do understand. You're concerned about my safety, and I understand that. I wish I could ease your mind, but I'm scared to death myself. We have nothing but unknowns here. We don't know what happened last time, and we don't know what will happen the next time. The chances are, however, the experience, whatever it is, will last about four hours. That's been its consistent history from the beginning."

They stood in the shadows of the edge of the room, their eyes locked, aware they were trying to talk sensibly about monstrous absurdities.

"You may be causing yourself irreversible genetic damage," she said finally.

"I don't think we are dealing with genetics in this instance, or even evolution, or any other biological concept of life. What happened—if it happened—is biologically impossible. In some way, I physicalized a hallucinatory experience, and despite its physicalization, it was a psychological event. We're beyond mass and matter here, beyond even energy. We're back before the first molecule, back before the first second of time. What we're back to is the first thought, the first conscious thought, the pure consciousness of creation. So I don't think there'll be anything like genetic damage. But I can't tell you nothing bad is going to happen, any more than an astronaut can reassure his wife he isn't going to flip off into space when he starts floating out there on the end of a silken string. But I must know, Emily. I must know if it happened, and if it happened, I must know why. An extraordinary event has occurred, and I must know why and how it happened. You're a scientist, so you must understand that."

"All I know is I'm your wife, and I'm scared to death."

"Don't make yourself responsible for this. There is nothing you can do that could stop me from repeating this experiment next week. It's too extraordinary."

"I've got a gut feeling something monstrous is going to happen!"

"All our evidence indicates nothing irreversible is going to happen. None of my experiences has lasted longer than four hours, and I have always reconstituted completely. There has never been any indication of any kind of damage at all."

"I'm trying to tell you I love you!"

"I know that. And I'm trying to tell you we are dealing with something so extraordinary I can't possibly ignore it or put it off. This is an all-bets-are-off sort of thing! We may be opening a black box that could scrap our whole picture of space-time! We might even have a link to another universe! For God's sake, Emily, you must know how I feel!"

She did know how he felt, of course. If she were in this situation, she would be no less obsessed. For some reason, this admission calmed her. She went to sit in the soft chair under the lamp. "Yes, I know how you feel," she said, "and I won't argue about it anymore. It's very late, Eddie. Would you like to stay here tonight? I could use the company."

He looked at her from the shadows of the room. "You said before you didn't want to confuse our situation."

She smiled bleakly. "I don't see how I could be any more confused than I am, and I could do with a little love and a little reassurance right now. You'll stay, won't you?"

"You know I want to," he said.

Friday night, April 30, was a befittingly Gothic night, a heavy rain whipping through the streets, lightning bleaching the medical school complex in flashes, sullen rumbles of thunder. Parrish got to the tank room around a quarter to six. Wearing his long white doctor's coat, he came in wheeling an examining table with an attached IV stand, which he had picked up from the Emergency Room. Clattering on the table were a marrow tray, a biopsy tray, a prep kit, a 35mm Nikon and a videotape setup, camera and console. Rosen-

berg, who was already there, helped him wheel the laden
table in. Rosenberg had brought his airline bag of tubes,
jars, drugs and syringes, his portable EEG stand, already
plugged in, and two standing gooseneck lamps. It all made
for quite a clutter.

"You got enough outlets in this room?" asked Parrish.

"Oh, sure," said Rosenberg. He examined the videotape camera. "I never used one of these."

"You just look and shoot, nothing to it."

With a grunt, Parrish sat down on the floor, leaning
back against the sound-attenuated wall, knees up. Rosenberg took a vial of sodium amytal out of the airline bag and
began mixing it.

"If push comes to shove," he said, "I'll give him a seven
hundred and fifty milligram bolus, is that what you want?"

Parrish, who had been staring blankly into space, said,
"What do you mean, if push comes to shove?"

"In case it happens."

"Yeah," muttered Parrish.

Emily and Jessup came in some twenty minutes late.
The Toyota had finked out on them, and they had had to
take a cab. They were soaked. Emily came in with a sopping
umbrella she was still shaking out. Parrish grumbled, "Why
don't you put your coats in the monitor room? There's
enough of a mess in here already."

Emily handed her raincoat to Jessup, who disappeared
into the monitor room with it. She paused by the examining
table and pointed to the IV bottle. "What's in this?"

"That's just some D_5E," said Rosenberg, pushing the
examining table and lamps against a wall. "We figure we'll

give him a big bolus of sodium amytal for starters. That's good for about twenty minutes. When it lightens, we figure we'll keep him on an amytal drip."

Jessup returned from the monitoring room, stripping off his shirt. "Listen," he said, "if this thing works and I come out of that tank anthropoid, I'm going to be in a very primitive consciousness. So if you're going to sedate me, the smart thing would be if you could inject me while I'm still in the tank. If this thing works, I'll be about four feet tall and standing up to my hips in water. I'll have a lot of trouble getting out of the tank, but once I get out you'll have to chase me down and subdue me. So if you can possibly medicate me while I'm still in the tank, that would be the best way to handle it."

"Okay," said Rosenberg.

Jessup went back into the monitoring room.

Parrish snorted. "I'll tell you this: if he comes out of that tank looking like an ape, I'm going straight over to Mass Mental and commit myself."

That was a few minutes after six. Twenty minutes later, Jessup went into the tank, and they turned off the overhead lights. They sat here and there around the room in the half darkness, leaning back against the soft, porous tiling of the sound-attenuated walls, hardly visible to each other except for their gray faces, growing bored as the evening wore on, falling into somber silences, talking desultorily in subdued murmurs. Every now and then, Parrish went to the tank and opened the hinged headpiece to check on Jessup. From deep within the square blackness that was exposed, Jessup's white face stared blankly out, framed, cadaverous, like a plaster cast sunk into a cushion of blackness.

The dark, silent vigil dragged on. They took turns going to the john, or taking a walk to ease their tension, always coming back to ask, "Did anything happen?" Nothing happened. One or another would suddenly get up just to stretch his legs. At one point, Emily interrupted a silence to say in a voice more frightened than even she expected, "Look—is there any way we can stop this? I'm getting really scared. I mean, what're we doing? We're screwing around with his whole genetic structure. I think we ought to stop this. I think we ought to call this off! Is it too late to call this off, Arthur?"

Parrish, who was fiddling around with the videotape setup, put it back on the examining table and went to the tank again, opened the lid. The white mask of Jessup's face lay in silent serenity in the blackness of the tank.

"Can you bring him down, Arthur?"

"Not unless he wants to, shall I try?"

Rosenberg got to his feet, went into the monitoring room, clicked on his mike and said, "How're we doing, Eddie?"

He waited for a response, but there was none.

Just before nine-thirty, Parrish came back from the john, his third trip. "Anything happen?" he asked the two shadowed forms sitting against the wall to the right of the tank.

"No," muttered Rosenberg.

Parrish shuffled to the tank again and raised the head section of the lid. This time he did not see Jessup's white face. This time he looked down into the sleeping mask of a somewhat gorilla-like face, its skin a black and shining hide. There was almost no brow, the close-cropped scalp hair coming down almost to the heavy simian ridge that bulged slightly across the brow. The facial fur was finer than that found on apes and did not entirely cover the ears. The lower part of the face was prognathic, the lips extended and open, revealing strong yellow but very human teeth. The eyes, even closed, were also more human than apelike, larger and not sunken into deep sockets. The neck, shoulders and that part of the chest that could be seen were covered with a fine short fur. Parrish stared a long stunned moment at this terrifying sight. "Oh, shit," he sighed.

From his seat along the wall, Rosenberg looked up. Parrish stood silently by the tank staring down into the black square of the tank.

"There is no way nohow," said Parrish softly, "that this can be explained on any physical level." He looked up to meet Rosenberg's questioning look. "Have you got your needle ready, Arthur? He said to try to nail him while he was still in the tank, didn't he?"

In the square of black below him, the eyelids of the creature were slowly opening, revealing malevolent little red eyes.

"Goddammit, Arthur," said Parrish, "bring your goddam syringe over here."

Rosenberg was instantly on his feet, syringe in hand. Emily didn't move. She remained sitting against the wall, tears streaking down her cheeks.

They did all the tests on him that had been planned.

Emily couldn't watch it. She spent the bulk of the next two hours pacing up and down the corridors of the basement of B Building. Now and then she would go into the monitor room and observe through the one-way window, but the sight of her husband in his dwarfed anthropoid state was intolerable and she could not look at his two best friends manipulating his sedated body as if he were nothing more than another lab animal. She could take perhaps ten seconds of observing all this and then, her nerves raw and agitated, she would stride out of the room and back into the corridors to pace and puff cigarettes.

First, Parrish and Rosenberg took pictures, two rolls of stills on the Nikon camera: full-size pictures, sectionals, pictures of the creature's curiously unformed feet, the unusually long, strong fingers of the furred hands, head shots, arm shots, leg shots. He had been stretched out on the examining table and hotly illuminated by the gooseneck lamps, while Rosenberg methodically focused his Nikon on one part of his body after another, muttering instructions to Parrish. "Okay, flip him on his side." Parrish would flip the slight body of the creature over. Parrish then shot videotape film of Rosenberg moving the creature's arms and legs to demonstrate as much of the musculature and mobility as possible.

Parrish and Rosenberg, needless to say, were both intensely excited, especially Rosenberg. Normally a soft-spoken, matter-of-fact, gentle man, he was now as breathless as a girl in love. He moved around the examining table, clicking his pictures, jabbering between clicks. "Listen, we've got to face this problem of a space-time link. This whole thing is time-linked somehow. I mean, why always this space on the evolutionary continuum? The drug somehow must have time-link constituents. It can't all be the consciousness. That has to be preposterous. Shit, Mason, we're into multidimensional time-spaces! I mean, this is post-Einstein relativity! This is explosive, Mason. Okay, Mason, flip him over, let's do the dorsal stuff!"

Parrish took some tissue samples, a procedure which required shaving a patch of hair off one haunch and pulling out a plug of epithelial tissue with a biopsy tool.

"His skin's black," Parrish muttered.

Rosenberg was moving around the room in a state of extreme agitation. He brought a jar containing a saline solution to Parrish so that the latter could empty his plug of tissue into it. "Look," gabbled Rosenberg, barely coherently, "what does it mean, I mean how do you define it, or even describe it? There are no coherent schemata for this. We're going to need a whole new language. All bets are off, man, all bets are off; we need a whole new space-time picture. We're in blue skies, baby, holy God!"

"Give me a gauze pad," said Parrish, who was ready now to stop the bleeding on the creature's thigh.

They took blood samples and EEG and polygraph tracings. "There's going to be a lot of diffuse slowing," said Parrish. "He's heavily sedated." They did a muscle biopsy and a spinal tap to get the CSF, and took the creature's blood pressure. When they were finished, it was nearly midnight. They withdrew the IV and laid the supine figure carefully on the floor. They cleared the tank room of all the equipment, wheeling the examining table, laden with everything they could pile on it, out into the corridor.

As they emerged, Emily, still distraught, said, "Is he all right?"

"I don't think you ought to come back in there," said Parrish. "He's fine, but the sedation is going to wear off in a couple of minutes, and we don't know what's going to happen."

Rosenberg, who was now bringing the EEG equipment into the hallway, added, "We don't know how long before he reconstitutes."

"If he reconstitutes," said Emily.

"The drug has a history of lasting only four hours," said Rosenberg. "He's always come down after four hours before. He says he reconstituted the last time after four hours."

"We never should have let him do it!" said Emily. "How did we let him talk us into this? This is crazy. None of us believed it would happen, that's why. We thought he was nuts, and we were humoring him. Oh God, something terrible is going to happen. Where is he now?"

"We've got him locked in," said Parrish. "We're going to put him back in the tank. That's what he said to do."

"I'm going back in with you," said Emily. She opened the isolation room door, and they followed her. She went into the monitoring room and watched the lumbering Parrish gently lift the small furry creature from the floor and return him to the coffinlike tank. They turned off the overhead lights, locked the tank room door and joined Emily in the monitoring room. Parrish, still wearing his long white coat, sank to the floor, bowed his head, closed his eyes. He was exhausted, drained. They all were. Rosenberg perched on his stool and rested his head on his arms, which were folded on the bank of monitoring equipment. Emily stood at the one-way window, staring into the semidarkness of the tank room. They had nothing to say to each other. Like Emily, the other two were both suddenly remorseful and frightened, awed by the incomprehensibility of the event in which they had just participated. Parrish was rank with sweat. Waves of chilled shivers swept over him. "I don't know," he muttered, more to himself than to anyone else. "I tell you I don't know." Rosenberg sat up wearily to stretch to the tape recorder and start the machine. The reels of the cassette began slowly to whir.

In the dark room beyond, the tank sat silent, an ominous black box. Then suddenly, simply, it blew up. There was an ear-shattering explosion of blue light that swept through the tank room in shock waves, and the four walls of the tank flew apart, as if a nuclear blast had been detonated inside it. Water geysered up to the ceiling in a screaming mushroom cloud, crashing with a clap as loud as thunder, and then flooded through the room to ankle depth. Infrared waves of light swept back and forth across the room, accumulating in intensity to oranges and yellows that seemed hotter than the sun, and the whole of the tank room flared molten with heat. Where the tank had been was a pulsating mass of white substance, rising out of the thin layer of boiling water, which must have been Jessup. An enormous gouge had been ripped out of the front of this grotesque white unformed thing, showing a section of skeletal structure. Emily screamed, beside herself with terror. Screaming, she lunged at the locked door that separated her from the tank room, and screaming, she tugged futilely to open it. Parrish and Rosenberg rose and stood crouched, petrified, staring through the window into the tank room.

In the middle of the blazing red tank room, the mass of substance seemed to be trying to assume a form. Stumps of arms and legs, misshapen and misplaced, bulged out of the mass and receded back into it. The substance itself changed color, began to bubble and boil as if being cooked by an interior fire. Deformed snouts and bleeding eyes appeared and disappeared. Then, for one startling moment, Jessup stood there sharply outlined, his human self, hands flat at his sides, a naked white statue of a man, which instantly turned into a baked, parched, mud-colored image on which thousands of tiny cracks appeared; and, for the briefest of moments, the figure looked as if it would simply disintegrate into dry dust. It began to scream so piercing and agonized a scream that it brought Emily's hysteria to an end. She unlocked the door and plunged inside, splashing to her husband in a room that had suddenly turned cosmic black, a blackness that pulsed with waves of force, shuddering bands of radiation. The room droned with the whir of energy. The space resonated and rippled. Jessup's form, still recognizably human, seemed to be caught in a pinch of energy waves and temperature differences, twisting and swirling around him, changing his coloration from luminous white to foggy infrared to the burning red of ultraviolet radiation to blurred chiaroscuro blacks and grays of the quality of x-rays. His form itself appeared to be dissolving in shimmering vibrations into the pulsating waves of energy penetrating him. Suddenly his body swelled until it distended into a sphere of gas, a shocking yellow gas turning red, and, as suddenly, collapsed in under the crushing weight of its own gravity. His bowels erupted into flames, rekindling the maniacal carnage of colors, now so phenomenally hot he was blinding white. He began to scream again in hideous terror, sinking to his knees as if he were melting, imploding as if he were being sucked into a black hole of his own. Emily flung herself upon the shuddering, increasingly shapeless antimatter of her husband and embraced him. Not fifteen seconds had elapsed from the time of the first explosion. Throughout, Parrish and Rosenberg remained staring, immobile, stunned to stupefaction.

In Emily's arms, Jessup's form throbbed and cracked and resonated, and he screamed his anguished primal shriek again. His eyes stared blindly out on some existential and unspeakable horror. Then the fluctuating extensions of matter that still retained the barely distinguishable shape of arms flowed out and enfolded themselves around his wife, and there they knelt together on the flooded floor of the room, two terrified figures alone in the dense black spaceless drone of energy, clutching each other against the horror of human origins.

As explosively as it began, it was over. The demented throbbing hum of entropic forces stopped abruptly. The cosmic black receded quickly as if it had been snatched up, and Emily held pressed against her the now entirely reconstituted naked form of her husband. They remained locked in their desperate embrace amid the wreckage of the tank room. Fragments of the wooden tank were everywhere, the smaller pieces floating listlessly in the several inches of water that covered the floor. Jessup was no longer screaming. There was no sound at all. The silence was palpable. After a moment, Emily looked down at the ashen face resting on her breast. She could feel his breathing so she knew he was alive, but he was manifestly in a coma. She turned her own harrowed face to the opaque window of the monitoring room and asked mutely for help. A moment later, Parrish and Rosenberg came in, disengaged Jessup's limp form from his wife and carried it into the monitoring room.

Beacon Hill
May 1976

They dressed Jessup and took him to his flat. All his vital signs were good, but he was still in shock. Parrish had to carry him to the car. Rosenberg stayed behind to clean up the mess in the tank room. Considering that only two weeks before, a still unaccounted for ape had been found in this same tank room, they decided not to invite questions by asking the building staff for help. Rosenberg was there till four in the morning.

Parrish and Emily put Jessup to bed, or rather made him comfortable on top of the spread, and then sat vigil in the living room. Parrish was reassuring. "His signs are all good. He'll probably sleep a day or two, come out of it a little stuporous. He's got a whopping load of drugs in him. It's not uncommon for a psychedelic experience to whack you out for a couple of days."

"You'd hardly call this just a psychedelic experience," muttered Emily, getting up to look into the dark bedroom. Her husband hadn't moved.

"His heart's good, his pulse is good, his pressure's good, his breathing's good. I'm more worried about you than I am about him."

"I'm all right, Mason."

She wasn't, of course. She was utterly shaken, beyond exhaustion. She tried to rest. She would sink into the soft chair, rest her head against the cushioned back, then suddenly be racked by a spasm of shudders and double forward with her head on her knees and cry. Every nerve end in her body was raw. When Parrish tried to place a comforting hand on her own hand, she startled like a doe, stood up. "Of all the goddamned men in this world," she cried out, "why do I have to love this one! I can't get him out of me! Do you know how many men I tried to fall in love with this past year? But it won't work! No matter whom I'm in bed with, I have to imagine it's him or nothing happens! No matter whom I'm eating with or walking with, there's always that pain because it isn't him! I'm possessed by him! It's crazy!"

"I think that's the way it's supposed to be," said Parrish.

"He doesn't give a damn about me."

"Oh, Emily, you're the only thing he really cares about outside his work."

She sat down, momentarily contained, but the sensation of hysteria was imminent. "No, Mason," she said, "he's a truth-lover, a God fucker. I was never real to him. Nothing in the human condition was ever real to him. Reality to Eddie is only that which is changeless, immutably constant. What happened to him tonight—that was Eddie's idea of love. That was consummation. He finally got it off with God. He finally embraced the Absolute, was finally ravished by Truth. And it fucking near destroyed him!" She was up on her feet again, yielding to the hysteria, screaming: "He never loved me! You knew him as well as I did! We were all bits of transitory matter to him!"

She flung herself down on the couch, where she sat rigidly, staring at the floor.

"You're going into shock. I'm going to give you something," said Parrish. He went into the bedroom, where he had left his little black bag, paused to watch the even rise and fall of Jessup's breathing. He came back into the living room, fumbling in his bag for a container of Valium. "This won't put you to sleep, but it'll take the edge off. I'll get you some water." He went into the kitchen.

A little after four, Rosenberg turned up. Emily was in the john, so Parrish answered the door.

"How is he?" asked Rosenberg.

"Same. She's a wreck though."

"Who isn't?"

"Did you get the place cleaned up?"

"Yeah. What a mess. Listen, I got all the stuff in my car, the tissue and blood samples, the film, the tapes. What do you want me to do with it?"

"Jesus, I don't know. We better stick the samples in the refrigerator."

Emily came out of the bedroom. "There's sandwich stuff and coffee in the kitchen if you want anything, Arthur."

"No, I'm okay. How're you doing?"

"I'll be all right. I called Sylvia to tell her not to worry about you."

"Thanks."

They sat around the living room, subdued, silent, having nothing to say really, still overwhelmed by the extraordinary events of the night. They had all the lights in the room on, the overhead lights and the two lamps, but it did little to relieve the tenebrous sensation that made the air around them dense. Every now and then, Emily would get up and look into the bedroom, but Jessup's condition remained unchanged. She would return to her seat and sip some tepid coffee, close her eyes, try to rest.

"Look," said Rosenberg suddenly, "it's got to be said. What the three of us witnessed tonight was one of the most fantastic instances in the history of science. Analogous perhaps to the first time somebody looked through a microscope lens and discovered solid matter wasn't solid. If I remember anything of my college physics, it was what the relativists would call a cosmic singularity. We've reached a point tonight where physical science just breaks down. We're in blue skies. We're star-trekking. Tonight was history, and what're we going to do about it?"

"I'm doing nothing about it," said Parrish. "Tonight scared the hell out of me, and all I want to do is go home and go to sleep and wake up and forget about the whole goddam thing."

"Maybe you're right," said Rosenberg. "Maybe we ought to drop it till tomorrow." He went into the kitchen for the purpose of slapping together a cheese sandwich, but he was back again before he had got one step out of sight. Obviously, he couldn't just drop it. "That tank just blew up. Whatever happened inside that tank released enough energy to blow open a wooden, aluminum-lined box. I don't know. Maybe there is something to this idea of a sort of human radioactive decay. Radioactive decay is always accompanied by a loss of quantum energy."

"For God's sake," Parrish flared, "let's drop the goddam thing! I don't want to talk about it!"

"I can't help it!" shouted Rosenberg. "You may want to go to sleep, but the way I feel right now, I don't expect to sleep for a year! I'm on fucking fire! I'm in there mopping up that goddamned tank room, and I've got to know why! Do you believe in supernatural agencies, Mason?"

"No!"

"Then what we saw tonight was a physical phenomenon, an inexplicable physical phenomenon, and if it's phenomenological, it's got to be explicable, and I've got to know why! Let me just talk, for Chrissakes! Let me just get it off my chest! I've been in there mopping up that tank room for three hours, and I want to tell you what I'd like to do. I'd like to take some of that tissue sample we took from Eddie, incubate some cells, treat them with the drug and move them through different force fields to see if there's any change in force. Then I'd like to x-ray—crystallograph the stuff, see if there's any change in structure. Then I'd like to get electron spin tests run off on the tissue, see if there's any

change in energy. Your pal Sproule could do all that for us.
Maybe he could take Kirlian photographs for us."

"What's all that going to do for us?"

"I'm trying to define the limits of the drug!" shouted
Rosenberg. "I go along with Eddie! I think the principal
force acting here is the consciousness! But, obviously, there
was some kind of interaction between the drug and the act
of consciousness! If we can define the limits of the drug in
this event, then we are beginning to localize the consciousness! How the hell else are you going to get at the
consciousness?"

"Arthur, I've had all I can take tonight! Just leave me
alone!"

"We've got to repeat this! We've got to repeat this with
other human subjects! We need a selective sample! We'll
put up a notice for volunteers in the Student Union, something like that, get five or six subjects, and just go back to
square one with them, step up the doses of the drug in a
graduated fashion, check them against Eddie's values! I bet
you we could even get a grant! We'll give them some kind of
bullshit about checking this drug for renal clearance, some
shit like that!"

"God almighty!" shouted Parrish. "This is Arthur Rosenberg talking, right? The conscience of the scientific community! The guy with all the petitions against genetic en-
gineering and protests against nuclear power! The big,
moral, science-for-the-people man! And here he is, ready to
test an untested drug on innocent humans! Hell, you're
ready to blow up your own best friend to satisfy your shitty
little need to know!"

"Who the hell are you yelling at? At least, I'm not closed to scientific hypotheses no matter how outrageous they are! I didn't burn Eddie's bathrobe with the goat's blood on it! If I ever told Eddie you'd burned his bloody robe, he'd kill you!"

"Please stop shouting!" cried Emily.

She moved quickly across the living room and into the bedroom, closing the door behind her. Inside the dark bedroom, she moved silently around the bed to the window, raised the shade and looked out into the sleeping dark backyards of the houses on the next street. After a moment, she turned to look at her husband on the bed. He had turned his head on the gray-shadowed pillow, his eyes were open, and he was looking at her. For a moment, she was immobilized by the fact that he was awake, and they just looked at each other. Then she knelt on both knees by the bed and examined his long, ashen face.

"How are you?" she murmured.

"Wiped out," he said in hardly more than a whisper.

"Would you like to go back to sleep?"

It took him a moment to gather the energy to answer. "Yes," he finally said.

"Would you mind if Mason had a quick look at you?"

"Good idea," he whispered.

His eyes closed in what seemed to be restful sleep. She struggled to her feet, started for the door to fetch Parrish, when she thought she heard her husband make some kind of noise. She turned quickly, and he was, in fact, saying something, barely more than mouthing it; in any event, she couldn't make it out. She came back around the bed, knelt again.

"I'm sorry, Eddie," she said in a voice hushed to match his. "I didn't hear you."

"I love you, Emily," he said, almost inaudibly.

She didn't know what to make of that, so she said, "I love you, Eddie."

He awoke again a little after six. The shade Emily had raised earlier was still up, and the first gray, passionless light of day filtered into the room, bringing with it a clement sanity, a sharpness of attributes, a comprehensible dimension. The apartment was utterly still, so still he could sense the presence of sleep in the living room. After a moment, he sat up, moved his legs over the side of the bed and stood. He was barefooted, wearing only his T-shirt and jeans. He moved around the bed to the door to the living room. Parrish and Rosenberg were obviously gone. His wife lay sleeping on the couch, one long white leg protruding from under a twist of blanket which was half on the floor along with a small puddle of her clothing, her blouse, jeans and sneakers. The blinds were drawn, and she seemed very white in the still darkness. Her face was drawn in pain. Her sleep was clearly not a pleasant one. He felt a rush of solicitude for her. He stood there staring at her from the bedroom doorway for what seemed a very long time. Then he absently wiped his cheek with the back of his hand and was startled to find that the sight of her had made him cry. He moved to the stuffed chair just to his right on the wall opposite her and sank down onto it, letting the sleeping stillness of the room encompass him.

She turned in her sleep, and what little part of the blanket that had covered her slipped down onto the floor. She curled up into herself, feeling the sudden chill of her nakedness, even in her sleep. He got up and crossed the room with the intent of restoring the blanket, but when he got there, he found himself lifting her head, squeezing onto the couch under her, taking her into his arms, warming her with himself. She shuddered and, still desperately asleep, began to whimper and cry, and sleeping still, she clutched at him suddenly out of the terror of her own nightmare, fevered by some frightened sensuality, making awkward, strangulated cries and arching panic-stricken up within his embrace, her cheeks streaked with tears, her eyes clenched closed, until she was sucking at his mouth with the rapacity of a vampire. He locked her in his arms and kissed her. Quickly the moment was over. Her head sank onto his chest, and she was instantly, innocently asleep.

She slept like that for two hours, slipping down after a while so that her head was pillowed on his thigh. He sat with his hands folded in his lap, occasionally looking down on her, mostly thinking. She was awakened by the phone ringing. "Oh, God," she sighed, slowly sitting up. "I hope it isn't the kids."

She got up and, naked except for her almost indiscernible panties, moved lithely across the room to pick up the phone, ending its third ring. She listened a moment. "Everything's fine, Arthur. He's fine. It's Arthur," she informed Jessup. "Are you fine?"

He nodded, admiring her gracile, shameless nakedness as she perched on the arm of the soft chair, trying to establish some order in her hair with her free hand. "No," she said companionably into the phone, "I was sleeping."

Jessup went into the kitchen, fetched a mug from the cupboard and poured coffee from the pot. He had had a cup of his own and a sandwich earlier. The makings were still on the table. He brought the coffee out to Emily, who was now sprawled in the chair, still on the phone, saying, "No, I don't know if he's eaten anything. . . ." She looked up at Jessup, smiled her thank you for the coffee, said, "Arthur, the indestructible Jewish mother, wants to know have you eaten anything?"

"Yes."

"Arthur," she murmured into the phone, "I'll call you back when I'm more awake. Everything's fine." She looked across at Jessup, now sitting back in the shadows of the corner of the couch on the opposite wall. "Is everything fine?"

He nodded.

"Everything's fine, Arthur. I'll call you back, okay?"

She returned the phone to its cradle, noted the sun fragmenting itself through the slits of the blinds. "God, what time is it? I should call the kids. Eddie, could you throw that blanket over here? I'm freezing."

"I love you, Emily," he said.

"You said that last night too, you know."

"I know."

"I think these have been the first unsolicited protestations of love you've ever made to me."

"I love you. I love the kids. I can't tell you how much

the three of you mean to me, how much I need you. I just wanted you to know that."

"Why don't you just come back to us?"

"It's too late."

He bent, picked up the fallen blanket, brought it to her, draped it across her and the chair. She said nothing, tried to read something in his shadowed face as he bent over her. Their eyes caught for a moment. She thought she saw pain and perhaps a shocking tenderness, certainly a sadness. He said, "I think it's too late. I don't think I can get out of it anymore." She almost understood what he was saying, and she felt afraid. The moment was intolerably fragile, and she looked away, afraid to shatter whatever was there. "I've committed myself to it," he said. "I don't think there's any way out. I thought perhaps I might burn all my files and research papers, something like that." He smiled briefly, distantly, as if he himself knew his words were, at least on the surface, foolish. He tucked the blanket around her and went back to the couch, to his dark corner, crossed his legs, stared at the floor.

She finally said, "That's kind of medieval, isn't it?"

"Well, I'm kind of medieval."

"Well, that's true." She looked away again, ferreting about in her mind for something to say, afraid to lose even this menacing connection between them. "Is it supposed to be some sort of an act of exorcism?"

"Yes. An evulsion of demons. I'm making it a religious act purposefully."

They regarded each other from opposite walls, the widening shaft of sunlight dividing them. He could see that the sudden religious flavor of his words had upset her. She was looking down at her coffee mug, being carefully silent, weighing her words, deciding whether to say anything.

"Look, I shouldn't have brought it up now; it was stupid," he said. "I didn't mean to make it sound so medieval and religious. I know it upsets you when my religious streak shows. The point I was trying to make, I think, was that what happened last night was more of a religious experience than a scientific one."

"Yes, I know."

"You saved me," he said. "You redeemed me from the pit."

"I wish you'd stop using all these biblical terms."

"All right. My matter was returning to pure energy, to a condition of pure nothingness. And you saved me from nothingness. But it doesn't end there, you see. It keeps going. Beyond nothingness to something even more horrible. Beyond the physical, beyond matter, beyond energy, beyond science. It keeps going. It never stops." He could hear his voice rising, and he paused to contain himself; he didn't want to frighten her. "You see, matter, energy, our whole universe, are not absolutes. They are all fictions of human consciousness. And there are other consciousnesses and other universes. Our space is just one space among infinite spaces. If you want to know what happens to a dying star, I can tell you—it is sucked into another universe, another consciousness. And if you hadn't held me in one piece, that's what would have happened to me. It is stark entropy and madness! It is stark terror! Can you understand what I'm saying?"

"Are you sure you want to talk about this now?"

"Oh, talking about it is nothing!" he cried out. "Hell, mankind has been talking about it forever, ever since the first human being noticed life was impermanent. We've sat in caves and speculated on shadows, stood on mountains and stared stunned at the infinite precision of the universe. We've seen visions, manufactured gods, probed, prayed, calculated, measured, wondered and dreamed. And for what? For something more permanent than human life. For some truth that stands immutably behind the silly, transparent superficies of human pain and human vanity and human greed and human savagery. Well, I found the fucker! I found the final truth all of us have been treasure-hunting for! I found it, touched it, ate of its flesh, drank its blood! I've seen it face to face, and it is hideous! It is insufferable! The pain cannot be described! I was in it, Emily! I was in that ultimate moment of terror that is the beginning of life! I can tell you what it is! It is nothing, simple hideous nothing! The final truth of all things is that there is no final truth! Truth is what's transitory. It's human life that is real! Truth is the illusion! Life is the only substance we have! I am truth; it is God that is fiction! This is real! You and me sitting here in this room! That is real! That is substance! That is the only truth there is!"

He emerged out of the cucullate shadows in the far corner of his couch and moved slowly to stand in the stripe of dust-moted white light that streaked across the floor from the slatted window. "I don't want to frighten you, Emily, but what I'm trying to tell you is that that moment of terror is not just a philosophical concept to me. It's a real and liv-

ing horror living and growing within me now, eating of my
flesh, drinking of my blood. It's real because I have made it
real. It's not just talk. It's alive. It's in me. It is me. And the
only thing that keeps it from devouring me is you."

"I think you're trying to tell me you love me," she said.

"I'm trying to tell you why I love you, that without you
I would have disappeared into unspeakable terror."

"I suppose that's why anybody loves anyone."

"For God's sake, Emily, don't be so facile!"

"I'm not being facile! My God, do you think you're the
only one who has experienced despair? The only one who has
felt the utter nothingness of life? We are all creatures of despair, Eddie! Life for all of us is a flight from the unspeakable terror! Life is an act of faith for all of us! That's why we
love each other! It's the only act of faith most of us are capable of! At least, it's the only act of faith I'm capable of."

"What I'm trying to say, Emily," he said, "is that despair is not just a matter of the spirit to me. It's a palpable
demon inside me, and it has to be ripped out."

"And so you want to burn your files."

"Yes."

She stood, pulling the blanket around her, chilled despite the widening shaft of sunlight stretching across the
room.

"As a penance? An act of contrition? Your private auto-
da-fé? You're going to drop your research, is that what it's
supposed to symbolize? You will no longer delve into forbidden mysteries. The repentant sorcerer. For God's sake,
Eddie, do you really think that after what happened last
night you're going to drop the whole thing, renounce your

life's work, spend the rest of your life piddling about with Milton Mitgang, testing the adrenal-thyroid output in schizophrenics? Do you really think that extraordinary mind of yours isn't going to wonder why it happened, how it happened, did it happen at all? If what happened last night happened, then you have just begun! You may have changed all our thinking about time and space and the very nature of reality! You're a brilliant scientist! You may be one of the great visionaries! Newton! Darwin! Einstein! Isn't that how you put it! You have opened one of the great black boxes of life, and nothing in this world or any other will keep you from exploring every mystery in it! You can't help yourself, Eddie. That's the way you are!"

"I can't live with it, Emily. The pain is unbearable."

"We all live with it. That unbearable terror is what makes us such singular creatures. We hide from it, we flee from it, we succumb to it, mostly we defy it! We build fragile little structures to keep it out. We love, we raise families, we work, we make friends. We write poems, we paint pictures, we build beautiful things. We make our own universe, our own truth, we believe in our own reality. And every now and then someone like you comes along who goes out to challenge it face to face. Passionate men. Poets, philosophers, saints and scientists. You're a man of extraordinary passion, Eddie. What the hell do you think makes me love you so much?"

"Listen to me, Emily. What happened to me last night can happen at any time—even now, right now, while I'm talking to you. That drug I've been using must have a latency factor. I don't know how much of it has accumulated in my limbic nuclei. It could be self-perpetuating. The chemical potential is there. I've attained a critical mass. Any act of consciousness could kick it off. Because whatever act of consciousness occurred last night is embedded in me just as much as the drug is. So it could happen at any time."

He was, she was shocked to see, crying. "Oh, God!" he cried out. "I'm sorry I brought this up, really. It wasn't what I wanted to say to you. All I really wanted to say this morning is that I love you. I just wanted to make you happy this morning. You are a marvelous thing, Emily. I just wanted you to know that I feel that way about you. But it's too late, you see."

He slowly raised his right arm and extended it for her to see. The vivid sunlight bleached it, made it look sepulchrally white. A bulge of protoplasmic substance was moving slowly up his arm under the skin like a mole. She stared, momentarily stunned. She sensed, then she heard a hum, a horrible resonating hum, the throbbing sound of the pulsing primal energy forces she had heard in the isolation room the night before.

"Defy it, Eddie!" she screamed. "You made it real! You can make it unreal. If you love me, Eddie, defy it!"

He was crying helplessly now, his cheeks glistening with the tears. His body began to rumble, crack and buckle as if forces inside it were about to break through the surface. He began to rapidly change shapes and forms, some recognizable, some merely monstrous. He seemed to have no more substance than a photograph, a projected illusion, a demented kaleidoscope of instant, transitory, transparent images flackering madly in the wide shaft of sunlight. The hideous hum had become insufferably penetrating. She clutched her ears trying to obliterate the sound, and closed her eyes tightly because she couldn't bear to watch any longer. When she opened them again, she saw a quick, fleeting image of her husband reaching out his arms to her for help, but she was petrified, utterly immobilized. The arms turned into stumps. She finally forced out the loudest sound she could manage, a sibilant hissing whisper, and then said, "If you love me, Eddie!"

She felt something within herself explode, a silent, painless pain of terror, and she clutched at her stomach, the blanket falling from her shoulders and slipping down to the floor at her feet. She knew what it was even before she looked down at her arms, which had begun to bulge and swell and discolor; a jagged crack appeared on her forearm and shot up the length of her arm as if it were splitting open. So the terror was now incarnate for her as well. She slowly forced her arm up so her husband could see. It was a stump, and even that stump was losing its definition as the lines that defined it became wavelike and seemed to melt her into the shrieking air. She was burning alive. She felt a massive shock just inside her skull above the eyes, a horrifyingly red-hot flame erupted within her. She could no longer see. She no longer had eyes, nor a mouth to scream with. She knew where she was going, to the lifeless, arctic, final desolation.

She thought she heard a scream, an echo of a scream, light-years away in the ultimate blackness, not quite a scream perhaps, rather a roar of rage, the fury of a raging animal. Her husband's human form, flickering in and out of the madness of all his other shapes, was reasserting itself. He was standing staring at her, a complete naked human form, but as immobile, emmarbled as a statue, stark white, and then, with a shocking wrench of effort, he began to move toward her, forcing humanness into himself. One step, two, he reached out to embrace the shapeless antimatter that was herself. She felt an enormous surge of emotion sweep through her, a remarkable joy.

It was over, instantly, abruptly over. The hum, the lunacy of illusion, the whole shattering moment, was done. They stood in the middle of the room, a slight, light-haired man of thirty-seven, beginning to bald just a bit but looking boyish at the moment in his jeans and T-shirt and bare feet, smiling, at least it seemed he was smiling; and a slim, gracefully naked young woman, her face pressed against his real body, her arms wrapped desperately around his real waist, a pair of young living human beings standing embraced in the white sunlight of their living room.

Acknowledgments

In the course of writing this book, I sought out and talked with dozens of scientists, who without exception gave of their time and knowledge with a generosity that can only be called extraordinary. I was also struck by the interest of these scientists in matters outside their disciplines—the humanities, for example. I confess I know few artists and writers who have an equivalent interest in the sciences. Yet, after two years of acquainting myself with contemporary science, it seems clear to me that art, science, religion and philosophy are all racing toward some common point of understanding. It has been a remarkable experience for me, the writing of this book, and for that I owe a great many people a great deal of gratitude.

I would like to thank Dr. Grover Farrish of Hyannisport, Mass., and Dr. Mary Stefanyszyn of the Harvard Medical School for helping me when I was first fumbling with the original ideas of this book, and for introducing me to that remarkable community of scientists in the Boston area—anthropologists, endocrinologists, the entire tissue-typing lab of the Harvard Medical School, and members of the school's psychophysiology department, especially Richard Surwit, Ph.D., now Associate Professor of Medical Psychology at the Duke University School of Medicine. I would also like to thank Charles Honorton, Director of Research of the Division of Parapsychology and Psychophysics at the Maimonides Medical Center Department of Psychiatry; and Shelby Broughton of Stockton State College who showed me my first isolation tank.

I acknowledge my deep appreciation to Dr. Harry L. Shapiro of the American Museum of Natural History; to Professor Eric Delson, also of the Museum and of Lehman College, CUNY; to David Post, Ph.D., of the Department of Anthropology at Columbia University; and to Professor Sol Miller of Hofstra University. I thank them all for the grounding they gave me in physical anthropology and paleontology.

I am grateful to Francesco Ramirez, Ph.D., of the Department of Human Genetics at Columbia University, for introducing me to molecular biology. Daryl E. Bohning, Ph.D., biophysicist in the Department of Medicine of S.U.N.Y. at Stony Brook, and Garrett Smith, Ph.D. in theoretical physics, of the Department of Philosophy at Fordham University, generously and patiently took me through some of the extraordinary beauty and philosophy of quantum mechanics. I also want to thank Drs. Ramirez, Bohning and Smith for reading the manuscript and offering me their counsel.

And most of all, I thank Jeffrey Lieberman, M.D., who funneled and clarified the mass of information that poured in from all these scientific disciplines. When he did not know the material himself, he found others who did, and then sat with me patiently explaining it all. I also want to acknowledge his support in those moments of despair when the sheer volume of requisite knowledge seemed to me more than I could ever master.

I am deeply grateful to you all.